SINFUL TRUTH

SINFUL TRUTHS BOOK 1

ELLA MILES

FREE BOOKS

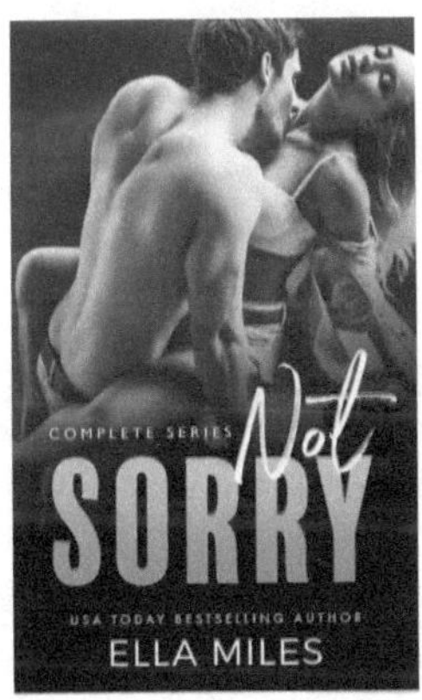

Read **Not Sorry** for **FREE**! And sign up to get my latest releases & updates here→EllaMiles.com/freebooks

Follow me on BookBub to get notified of my new releases→Follow on BookBub Here

Join Ella's Bellas FB group to grab my **FREE** book **Pretend I'm Yours**→Join Ella's Bellas Here

TRUTH OR LIES WORLD

TRUTH OR LIES SERIES:

Taken by Lies #1
Betrayed by Truths #2
Trapped by Lies #3
Stolen by Truths #4
Possessed by Lies #5
Consumed by Truths #6

SINFUL TRUTHS SERIES:

Sinful Truth #1
Twisted Vow #2
Reckless Fall #3
Tangled Promise #4
Fallen Love #5
Broken Anchor #6

PROLOGUE
ZEKE

I ALWAYS KNEW I would die young.

I've known it since birth. From a young age, I would take the blame for Enzo, my closest friend later turned boss. He was always pushing the limits, stealing things he could've bought with a snap of his fingers. He was horrible at thievery, so he always got caught. But I took the blame. Most of my childhood was spent in detention—for every wallet, purse, and laptop Enzo stole just because he could. The man has more wealth than a small country, but it doesn't stop him from showing his power, even from a young age. And I protected him at all costs.

Langston, my best friend and brother in every way that matters, got in trouble in different ways. He preferred to let his fists talk for him—something I understood quite well. We got in more fights than should have been allowed. We both should've been expelled from school, but because of our association with Enzo, no man, not even our principal, would do more than give us detention.

Both men I've protected my entire life. Enzo and

Langston are both taller and stronger than any other man I've ever met. But neither man compares to me.

I'm not bragging; I'm humble to my core. But at six foot five, I tower over both of them. My muscles ripple from my body, and men cower at my feet with one glare—a look I've perfected over the years. Yet deep inside, my heart aches to be warm, gentle, anything but the beast I appear to be on the outside. But to anyone except Langston and Enzo, that's what I am—a beast.

My straggly hair and scruffy face only add to that notion. My tattoo ridden body adds fire to my bad boy image. I almost never have to actually use my fists and body to protect my boss, Enzo Black, or rescue my dipshit friend, Langston, when he's in trouble. My appearance more than does enough to scare the shit out of any foe.

But this time was different.

This time wasn't about fighting to keep them safe; this time, I had to sacrifice everything to protect someone more worthy of my protection.

Enzo is my boss; I vowed to protect him with my life the day I took the job at eighteen. After growing up as practically brothers, I would have sacrificed my life for his for free. But this time he didn't ask me to. He asked me to protect another—one more valuable to him than his own. A woman who rests so deeply in his heart that he will never be able to get her out. A woman whose love consumes him.

Kai Miller—a woman I myself love. *No, I'm not in love with my best friend's girl.* Just in love with her strength, courage, and warrior attitude. I'm in love with the way she loves him.

I once thought I was in love like that. But after seeing it, seeing their love grow right in front of my eyes, I know I never have, nor ever will, experience a love like theirs.

Because this is where my story ends—saving the girl. I stepped in front of a bullet for her. The evidence is blood leaking from my chest as my heart pounds over and over and over—each time spilling more precious drops of blood until I'm bled dry.

You would think I would regret my decision to save a woman I didn't love. That I should've reserved this moment for the woman that had captured my own heart instead of the woman destined to be Enzo's equal in every way.

But I don't regret it even now.

My only regret is not knowing if it was enough. *Did I save Kai? Or did I fail? With my death, will she be safe or left vulnerable?*

I will never know the answer. Unless perhaps in heaven, I can look down upon her and see that she survives stronger than ever.

Who am I kidding? If an afterlife exists, I won't be going to heaven; my sins will take me straight to hell.

But then, I'm already in my own personal hell.

The bullet knocked me out, but I became conscious again when the storm pushed me over the railing of the yacht and into the water. The last thing I remember before going underwater was the splash of the salty ocean on my face—then nothing.

How I survived this long, I don't know. But I survived long enough that the yacht my friends were on is no longer here. There is no wreckage for me to cling to. No lifesaver floating in the water. I am stuck in the middle of the fucking ocean in the middle of the fucking night—blackness surrounds me.

I should feel alone. But I'm not. I would prefer to be alone. I would prefer to die quietly and calmly by myself. Even though I did my best to protect those I cared about, I never wanted a martyr's death. However, that is exactly what I'm going to get.

Every nudge of the waves reminds me that I'm not alone here in the ocean. That below me are hundreds of sea creatures all doing their best to survive. That sharks and other deadly creatures could be hiding, inching closer every second, being lured to me as my drops of blood seep into the ocean. Every second that passes is another second closer to death. *But will I die alone, going quietly into the ocean from loss of blood, or will I die violently fighting a shark until the bitter end? Or will the waves finally overpower me, until I drown?*

I tread water with my aching legs, my arms too painful and sore to move. My right arm clutches to my chest, trying to keep as much blood inside my body as possible.

The stars twinkle overhead, taunting me with their beauty and ability to stay alive for so long. My life was short, fleeting. I barely made a blimp on this world. But the stars, they shine forever in a thick layer of darkness draping over us all. They do not fear death; they welcome it. Because even in death, the stars continue to shine for sometimes thousands of years later.

I know my death will be the same. What was taken granted before—the friendships, the brotherhood, will be turned into more. But I only hope it gives Enzo and Langston the strength to face our enemies. And I hope once they're safe, they can move on.

I continue to tread water as each second passes by in what seems like an hour, so slowly I'm not sure I'm moving at all. I should be grateful; these are my last moments on this earth. Despite the pain I'm feeling in my body, the beauty of the night being stranded in the middle of the ocean doesn't go unnoticed. The moon creeps up higher in the sky—a full moon that turns the dark skylight.

The moon will be the last thing I see before I close my eyes—before I die.

I can already feel myself fading—my will to live leaving my body as my legs tire beneath me. My breathing is slow and heavy; my lungs are filling with a little saltwater each time I try to breathe. I'm not able to fully keep my head above water any longer.

This is the end. The end of my story. And what a sad story it was.

No!

My story wasn't sad; I did what I always thought I would do—give up my life to save another. One more worthy, one meant to change the world. And Kai Miller will change the motherfucking world.

My long hair falls over my eyes, but I don't have the energy to brush it off my face so that I can stare up at the beautiful sky. And one of my last acts before sacrificing my life was giving a scrunchie to Kai to keep her hair back so she could fight without worrying about her hair in her face.

I smile, thinking of that moment. And how it felt to do something so simple and kind for a woman so amazing as Kai. I lived for moments like that. I just never got to have those moments with a woman I was in love with.

I close my eyes, deciding it's better this way, that blackness sends me to my death instead of looking at the hair in my eyes. My throat makes a strangled sound as more water enters my chest. I've always loved the ocean, dying in it doesn't seem like such a bad idea. I'd rather die here than be buried on some hillside with a tombstone that my friends feel compelled to visit and bring flowers and all that bullshit. This way, I'll just be gone.

Maybe they'll think of me the next time they are on the ocean, feel me in the wind that blows through their hair, but that's it. They won't feel obligated to me in any way other than just living their lives.

The pain starts, and the panic sets in as my lungs continue to fill more and more with saltwater instead of the oxygen they desperately desire.

I may let the ocean take me, but I don't want to drown. I want my death to be easy and quick, as do all humans. So I remove my hand from my chest, letting the blood spill quicker from my wound. But I think the saltwater—the very thing that's trying to kill me by drowning me—is also saving me. Because my blood should be flowing much faster from my chest. Instead, the water pressure is keeping the blood within my veins.

Dammit.

I kick harder, determined to die at least on my own terms. I try to get my chest above the water, I try floating on my back, but the waves fight harder, pushing me back under.

No, I will not let you win.

I force my legs to kick, my arms to paddle; I urge my body to float. *Dammit, float!*

But my heavy body doesn't have the buoyancy to float. My arms are exhausted, barely doing more than a toddler would who has just learned to splash in a pool of water. My legs carry all my strength—but my strength floated away with Kai, and Enzo, and Langston. My strength is still on that yacht. My strength is gone.

The pain is the only thing keeping me alive. The agony triggers adrenaline—the need to survive deep in my body. But I don't want to survive, not like this. I don't want to spend hours more floating in this water waiting for death to come.

So much for quick and painless.

My death may not be painless, but it will at least be quick. I'm done suffering. And I know I have enough willpower left in my body to die on my own terms.

Drowning it is.

I take a couple more deep breaths, trying to get one or two moments of comfort, security, and warmth inside my body before I take the plunge, but when you're dying, even that simple breath of oxygen isn't comforting. It's pain and pain and pain. It is all I feel. It is all I think about—the pain.

I've never been one to fear death, and I won't let myself be scared right now. Even if I could feel fear, the pain wouldn't let me—my body trembles as my muscles fatigue. My chest makes an awful wheezing sound with each anguished breath. My eyes burn as more saltwater enters them. And my heart—my heart pumps harder and more distressed with each thump, trying to decide between holding on and giving out as the pain possesses my body.

It's time.

My body switches from trying to survive to just trying to get rid of the pain. I need to end; the suffering is too much. So I take one more big breath, and then I dive under the heavy waves and into the darkness.

Death should come quickly but not painlessly. I have to endure more torment in order for the pain to stop. But right now, with every nerve-ending in my body begging me to make it stop, it's a trade-off I will gladly endure.

Deeper into the darkness, I descend.

Deeper.

Deeper.

Deeper.

I force myself to kick as hard as I can to get as deep as I can because I know that once my lungs start filling with water, my fight or flight response will kick in again, and I'll try to save myself. And I can't handle any more moments of pain.

With each kick deeper, I feel my lungs tightening, the pressure constricting around my body, intensifying the discomfort.

Just a little further, I think.

If I can get just a little deeper, I won't be able to get to the surface fast enough when I start to panic. This is the end, being surrounded by nothing but water, darkness—alone.

But then I feel it, a jolt in my body, a reverse in direction. Instead of traveling deeper into the depths of the ocean, I'm making a break for the surface.

What the hell?

I have no idea what's happening. *Did my body spontaneously change directions? Or am I already dead, and an angel is grabbing me and taking me to heaven?*

I don't know, but I don't have the strength to fight it. So I let whatever force is pulling me back toward the surface do its job.

Time moves fast again as I hit the surface. My mouth opens, gasping for air, getting just enough oxygen to keep me firmly on the side of living instead of dying.

I feel a hand over my face sweeping the wet mop of my hair clear from my eyes and mouth, making it easier to breathe. I don't know how I'm staying afloat because I'm not kicking or treading water, I'm completely dead weight.

But once the hair is gone from my face, I hear a sigh relief.

I open my eyes and come face-to-face with my savior. *And what a face it is.* Striking brown eyes loom into mine, examining my face quickly and thoroughly to ensure that I am alive and not dead. Long dark hair frames her face parted perfectly down the middle, like a model coming out of the water instead of the sea monster I must look like. Her red lips pout, disappointed in something she sees in me. But all I can think is her lips are magical.

This can't be real. I must be imagining some perfect woman in my last moments here on Earth. I'm not really here; I'm still deep within the heart of the ocean. But if my fantasies are going to try to give me one last moment of pleasure before I leave this earth, I'm not gonna fight them.

The woman grabs my arm harshly and jerks me toward her.

"Come on," she says.

Come on? I'm not sure what she expects me to do, I have no energy to swim, there is no way I can save myself; I'm drowning in the middle of the ocean with no boat, island, or person to save me. But I let her pull me, assuming she's a current dragging me deeper into the ocean, waiting until my lungs give out.

She pulls hard, and I feel my body moving, dragging behind her. I don't know where we're going or what she wants me to see before I die, but it seems urgent. Probably because she knows I only have seconds left to live. Maybe it's something beautiful like a seahorse or whale or dolphin— something beautiful she wants me to see before I die. But all I can think is that there's nothing more beautiful than her.

She swims harder now, more determined than before. But I'm not desperate or hurried, not in the final moments. I study everything about her. The way her arm darts into the water with beautifully tanned skin that shows just how much time she spends in the sun. I watch her toned legs kicking with the efficiency of a dolphin. I watch her ass bob up and down over the waves in bright red bikini bottoms.

If only she were real. If only I found a woman like her while I was still living.

But then Kai would be dead. There would've been no one there to save her if I had fallen in love with a woman like this. Because there's no way I would've sacrificed myself to save a friend when I had a woman I loved who desperately needed me to live. Maybe that's why I never found love. Because it would've made me a worse version of myself.

"Can you help me at all, you big oaf?" The woman says, throwing her head over her shoulder, shooting daggers with her eyes in my direction.

I smile. I don't know why the woman is so angry at me, but I devour the look on her face.

When I don't move to help her, she huffs and then starts kicking wildly again, lugging me along behind her.

I see the sky changing from dark to light. It must be the light that everyone talks about seeming just before they die. And I know my time is almost up.

The woman sees it as a sign to swim faster in the water.

Until she suddenly stops.

I don't care why she stops. With us no longer moving, I can study her features more clearly, I can see the light freckles dusting over her nose, I can see the gold flecks in her otherwise dark brown eyes, I can see the streaks of red in her hair as the sun catches it just right, as it begins to rise over the horizon behind her.

And I know in this moment she is my angel. She is here to take all of my pain away. And I'll forever be thankful for her.

She shakes her head at me again, disappointed, but I don't understand why.

She reaches for something behind her, and my gaze runs along her tanned arm to the tip of her red painted fingernails as she grips the first rung of the ladder.

A ladder?

She hosts herself out of the water, dragging me to the ladder behind her. I grip on automatically, and then I'm pulled into a boat.

We both fall to the wooden deck, exhausted and panting heavily.

"I don't know why I risked my life to save you when it's clear you wanted to die," she says.

"Die?" I ask.

She nods. "You dove under the water just as I shouted that I was going to throw you a lifesaver."

My eyes widen. I have no idea what she's talking about. I never heard her speak before I went under.

Her eyes soften as she realizes I didn't hear her. I was just an anguished man, who was tired of the pain and needed to end his life on his own terms.

She quickly looks over my body until she sees the blood oozing from my chest where the bullet hit me. She grabs for a towel behind her and holds it to my wound, applying pressure with her hands.

"Is this real?" I ask. *Or is this the end? The pressure of the ocean squeezing out the last drops of oxygen from my lungs?*

"This is real. You are on my sailboat off the shores of Saint Kitts. We can make it back to the island in about two hours if the weather is in our favor. Do you think you can hold on that long, sailor?"

I nod.

She gives me the faintest hint of a smile or at least what I assume for her is a smile. Her lips thin, her eyes turn bright, and her cheeks shade pink.

"You're my angel," I say.

She shakes her head. "I'm no angel."

"What's your name?"

"You can call me Siren."

Siren—such a beautiful, unique name. A name that for thousands of years meant death to any sailor who met a siren. But this woman isn't like the mythical stories. This woman saved my life.

I close my eyes, needing rest.

She strokes my face, running her hands through my long hair.

She starts humming, and it's the most beautiful sound I have ever heard. Calming, entrancing, enduring. If I could stay awake, I would, just to listen to her voice.

"I shouldn't have saved you," she says. But then she's right back to humming and singing with her heavenly voice.

She's wrong. I will make her see that risking her life was worth it. She saved me. Now I owe her. And I never relent on a debt.

1
———

SIREN

THREE MONTHS LATER

I WAS RAISED to tell the truth, no matter what. It should be my greatest virtue. Instead, I consider it my greatest weakness. Maybe it's because of how I learned the skill that makes me feel this way. But the truth of the matter is that I can't lie.

Can't—as in can't physically make my mouth form the words to tell a lie. I know that's hard to believe, but it's my truth.

It started when I was three. My best friend in the world at the time, Gavin, ripped my favorite doll out of my hands, so I pushed him. He ended up crying for the next twenty minutes, loudly enough that my father came to check on us. When he asked me what happened, I lied. I said he had fallen and hurt himself, not because I pushed him. That was my first lesson, my first mistake.

What my three-year-old self didn't realize was that my father had been listening to Gavin and me fighting in my bedroom behind the door. He heard me shove him. He knew I wasn't telling the truth. And I paid for my sin, dealt by my father's belt.

At three, I didn't quite realize what sinning was, but over the years, my pastor father and religious mother drilled the message into me. Lying was a sin equal to murder in their eyes. Whether it was the smallest of white lies or biggest of lies, it made no difference in their eyes.

It was a sin.

I was a sinner.

And so I had to be punished.

But I also learned another important lesson in those first few years of life; I'm not a fast learner. The daily beatings did nothing to stop my lies. I didn't lie about anything big— just normal childhood fibs.

Did I eat a cookie before dinner? No, I lied. *Slap.*

Did I finish all my homework? Yes, I lied. *Slap.*

Did I drink alcohol at the party? No, I lied. *Slap.*

And over and over again. *I lied. I sinned. I was punished.*

It took me almost eighteen years to finally learn my lesson. Eighteen years of groundings, spankings, beatings. Eighteen years of being wrecked and broken—until the lies finally stopped.

I can't lie now, even as a thirty-two-year-old woman. I got pulled over for speeding last year. When the cop asked me if I knew I was speeding, I said yes. I couldn't lie, I couldn't fib and say that I didn't know the exact speed I was going. I said I knew I was going exactly twelve miles over the speed limit. I got the ticket.

But it's not all bad. Telling the truth has saved me as many times as it's gotten me into trouble. For example, when I was twenty-one, my boyfriend at the time and I went through an adventurous sex phase. We tried all the toys, positions that we could find. One drunken night my boyfriend thought he was shoving a dildo into my ass turned out it was a spiked paddle. I bled, we got scared and ended up in the emergency room. Normal, rational people might fib, embarrassed by the truth. But I told them exactly what happened and got medical care much faster.

But sometimes a lie could save me, even from the smallest of things. When my friend, Rue, asked me how her butt looks in her new dress, I told her the truth—it makes her butt look too big. Times like those, I wish I could lie. I wish I could spare her feelings, my cheek when she slaps me, and the turmoil our friendship goes through every time I tell her the truth when she's looking for me to lie.

It's my burden, my curse, and my greatest strength.

My sailboat floats into the harbor of Saint Kitts with just me aboard. It's a beautiful day, but *why do I have a sinking feeling in my stomach every time I come back here?*

I try not to focus on the feeling in my gut; after all, I've learned not to trust it. It's led me in the wrong direction many times before.

I tie off my sailboat, and then I hop down to the shaky pier. The wood beneath my sandaled feet is worn, the paint stripped from the harsh weather here. Each step I take, the wood creaks, the pier sways. All it would take is one mediocre storm to wash this all away. Yet, somehow day after day, year after year, the pier and the small town relying on it, remains.

I strut down the pier with my bag thrown over my shoulder. Even though I've been a resident of this island for years, it doesn't stop the men's eyes from stalking me as I walk.

Each gaze says something different.

I want you.

I'm imagining you naked.

You don't belong here.

This is a man's world.

I've learned not to let the inappropriate stares and whispers bother me. There was a time I would have pummeled each and every guy who dared to look at me or comment about my appearance. But I've learned it's not worth my time. Sometimes, my body is even an asset.

I've considered dressing more conservatively, at least when I'm here. But that's not who I am. And honestly, I like the stares. The stares expose each man's true self. They tell me the men I should stay away from. They tell me the honest men from the pigs.

My clothes are a test. My jean shorts barely contain my ass; the front pockets hang lower than the hem. My cut-off shirt reveals my tanned stomach and dips down, showing my more than adequate cleavage. And my hair is loose in a long mane of thick waves. The island is windy, and my brunette locks are constantly in my face. But when I flip my hair, it's the ultimate test. The men can't resist a good hair flip. It's like I'm calling out to them, alerting them to a hot female in their presence. And every man on the pier failed.

I smirk as I walk off the pier with my duffel bag over my shoulder. I find my white 1980 Toyota Land Cruiser parked right where I left it three months ago when I was last here. Three months—such a long time, but it also feels like no time has passed at all.

I prefer the sailboat to the island. The ocean is unpredictable; you never know if you will live or die. You have to constantly be on your guard. You have to be prepared for anything.

I unlock my car and toss the duffel bag in the back seat.

I guess life on the island is the same. Each day is a struggle to live. On the ocean, it's just me and the water.

Here—there is more than one danger I have to deal with. The men on the island are my biggest threat.

I climb into the driver's seat and turn the key in the ignition, which, I'm happy to say, starts. I've come back from many trips when the car wouldn't start. Or it was stolen. The fact that it starts is a win. I back out of the beachside parking lot. It's one of only three free spots you can park in long term.

A shadow crosses in my rearview mirror. I slam on the breaks to avoid hitting the tall man standing behind my car.

"Shit."

I grip the wheel like my life depends on me hanging onto the wheel. I pant heavily as beads of sweat form on my forehead. I run my hand through my hair, changing the direction of my part from left to right. And then I let my eyes flicker up to look into the rearview mirror and pray I didn't hurt the man. Hopefully, he's still standing.

But when I look into the rearview mirror, I don't expect what I see.

The man is still there, but his face is only barely visible in the mirror. He towers over my SUV. He's standing in ripped jeans and a snug white T-shirt that barely fits his bulging biceps. His body is tall, fit, and rugged. But that isn't what draws me to him. His face does. It's a face I've seen before. Dark scruff clings to his chin, not in the messy I-don't-care-what-I-look-like kind of way that most men on the island wear. His looks like it is a part of him. It's tidy and neat. His hair is pulled back into a messy man bun. Not something I would usually be attracted to, but on him, his hair brings out the beast below the surface. But his eyes are what have me captive. I recognize the brown ambers of his eyes.

The same eyes I pulled from the ocean a little over three months ago.

He's alive.

I wasn't sure if he would make it. When I pulled him from the water and saw the damage his body had been through, I was afraid I would arrive in town with a dead man in tow. Somehow he hung on, even though he was clearly hallucinating. He called me his angel. But I don't think he meant that I was an angel because I saved his life. At one point, I think he actually thought he was dead, that he was in heaven, and that I was a real angel.

But this man lived long enough for me to get him to the island. I shoved him in the back of this very beater. I glance at the backseat that is still stained red with his blood. No matter how much scrubbing I did, I couldn't get it out. I knew for sure he was going to die as I drove him to get medical help. But again, he proved me wrong. For a man so intent on dying when I first jumped into the water to save him, he sure as hell fought to live once I pulled him out.

Even though he survived the hours it took to get to the island, the car ride to get medical help didn't mean he was out of the woods. Our small hospital doesn't have the same level of equipment and care most hospitals have. It wouldn't have been enough to save him. Which is why I didn't drive him to the hospital. I drove him into danger, but it was the only way I could think of to save his life.

And it paid off. The man is alive. Despite me almost running him over with my car. *How ironic would that be?* It took every ounce of energy and determination I had to save him three months ago, only to run him over with my car and kill him in a split second now.

I never thought I'd see him again. I thought one of two things would have happened by now. He'd either be dead or gone. No one stays on this island long term if they know what's good for them. They flee the first chance they get. Sure, tourists always say they'd love to live here. But they don't really mean it. The island is paradise and hell. Its beauty draws men in, only to torture them with regret as soon as they make the island their home.

So what is the man still doing here?

What was his name again?

I pushed his name from my mind. I knew I couldn't keep his name in my thoughts. His name would haunt me. When I saved him, I knew there would be unforeseen consequences of my actions. It hasn't happened yet, but it will.

Enzo?

Kai?

No, neither was his name. Just names he muttered in his sleep.

The man's eyes cut to mine, and I think he remembers me as his head tilts to the side to try and study me better. But he can't see me, at least not enough of me to make a positive ID. My windows are tinted to help keep the burning sun out of my car and so I can't be seen.

He can't see me.

But maybe he senses the change in the air—the familiar unease growing in my belly with him near. I don't know why everything changes with this man near. And not in a good way. I've never felt my pulse race so quickly, my stomach flips in unsettling ways, and I'm nibbling nervously on my bottom lip, like that is somehow going to help.

"Zeke," one of the men from the pier shouts in our direction.

Zeke—that was his name. It fits him. It's a powerful sounding name. And he must be a powerful man to have survived this long. The island wears people down, but he looks better, stronger. I study him closer, trying to decide if he has money. His clothes don't give me any designer, rich person vibes. The man shouting for him is just a fisherman who doesn't make a lot of money. All the signs say he is nothing. Probably doesn't even have enough money to buy a plane ticket off the island. Or maybe he has amnesia and doesn't know where to buy a plane ticket to? Or even how to access his bank account?

No.

This man doesn't carry himself like he doesn't know who he is. He stands tall and proud. The twinkle in his eye tells me he's a man that likes to laugh and live well, yet he prefers to use his size to intimidate any person he perceives as a threat. The look now is meant to tell me to back off, that he could kill me with his fists alone. I don't doubt that he could, but I also see the softness in his eyes. It's a deadly combination. He can make any man fall to his knees in fear, while every woman would fall to their knees in front of him for a very different reason.

Zeke knows exactly who he is. He's a burly man who knows how to use his body to get what he wants. I can't imagine a man like him doesn't have money.

So what is he still doing in a place like this?

"Zeke, you coming?" the man on the pier asks.

Zeke nods but doesn't stop looking through the rear of my car straight to my soul.

He can't see me. He can't see anything.

Finally, Zeke looks away and starts walking toward the pier.

I exhale a breath, pushing the air too quickly through my lungs, so it almost hurts to breath. And then I zip out of my parking spot, trying to put the events behind me. I can't think about Zeke. I can't think about anything other than my job.

But I can't help but glance in my rearview mirror as I drive away from one of the most attractive men I've ever seen. A man I can't read. *Is he a good or bad man?*

Who am I kidding? All men are bad. I've learned that lesson enough times by now. Even the good ones have an evil streak. Even the good ones will damage my heart until it is no longer recognizable. Until my heart is no longer mine.

Thump-thump.

Thump-thump.

Thump-thump.

Damn, stupid heart speeding up just thinking about Zeke.

My heart still hasn't learned its lesson. Not that I have a heart left to give. My heart is no longer mine. I haven't had anything truly mine in a very long time, including my own body.

But it doesn't stop my heart from yearning. From yearning to know more about Zeke. To wondering if he could be the one—the one who is different. The one who could stop my pain. The one who could save me.

Ha—I don't need saving. I chose this life. I want this life. Any other life would make me weak and vulnerable. My life makes me strong.

I've already chosen my fate. I know how my story ends.

Saving Zeke was a mistake, I know that as I watch his shadow disappear from view. He wasn't just any sailor who wasn't experienced enough and fell victim to the sea—he's different. He's going to wreck my perfect little world, blow it up in a way I'm not prepared for.

Saving a man should absolve me of my sins. But instead, saving him will cost me everything.

2

ZEKE

I CAN'T SHAKE the strangest feeling as I walk down to the pier. I'm not even sure what my body is reacting to. *The beat-up Land Cruiser almost hitting me?*

No, that was hardly life or death. The car stopped long before it got close to me.

But I can't shake the déjà vu feeling. Maybe because I've passed that beat-up SUV parked along the beach every day I've been coming to work. And to see it actually move put me into shock. *Yea, that has to be it.*

I stare down at my arms, where goosebumps have formed, and hair is sticking straight up as if warning me that danger is nearby.

I glance back as the car speeds off down the highway.

There can't be anything dangerous about a person who can barely afford a car. Most people think that poor people are more dangerous than rich. That poor people are desperate and addicted to drugs. That they will do anything to survive. Anything to get the drugs—not true.

Sure, poor people can be dangerous. And yes, some are addicted to drugs. Stealing petty amounts of money or robbing someone at gunpoint, if they happen to get ahold of a gun, is the most damage they can do. Yes, that might end in a death or two, but it's nothing compared to the damage a rich person can do.

A rich person has more to lose, and that makes them more dangerous. A rich person can hire an army to take out the threat. They have endless weapons at their disposal. They can pay off the police to ensure there are no consequences for their actions. Rich people can make anything they want happen. I know—I've worked for a rich person my entire life. I've seen what wealth can get you.

Whoever was in that car was not a threat. Whatever fucked up spidey sense my body was trying to use to warn me is broken.

"Zeke, get your fucking ass over here if you want to get paid!" Wayne says.

I shake off the strange feeling and continue walking to the pier. I don't speed up my steps. That's not who I am. I may follow orders, but I don't change who I am. I'm the gentle giant—calm in the face of fear. And I don't like being disrespected. I don't like working for bosses I don't admire. And Wayne has not earned my respect.

"What do you want, Wayne?"

"It's Mr. Hill."

I stand, towering almost a foot taller than him. My muscles ripple and contract in ways his never will. He may write my paycheck, but I'm not going to pretend I won't kill him if he fucks me over.

"What task have you arranged for me today, Wayne?" I ask, continuing to use his first name.

He frowns but doesn't fight me on it. An audience has formed around us as his men stop their work to watch our inevitable fight.

I still don't understand why Julian Reed has Wayne as his number two. I haven't learned everything there is to learn about Julian, but I do know he's smart, powerful, and ruthless. He's a lot like my old boss, Enzo Black. He just doesn't have quite the empire or money that Enzo has. His money is newer. His empire is just starting out and focused mainly on selling drugs as far as I can see. While Enzo has his hand in everything.

"I need you to load the speed boat with the cargo from the truck. Think you can handle that before lunch?" Wayne says, his eyes threatening to fire me. He hates me. If it were up to him, he'd have already fired me—*do us both a favor.* But it's not up to him. It's not even up to me. I was saved. I owe a man my life—something I can never repay. But I'm doing my best before returning to my real life.

"It will be done within the hour," I answer.

"No way. You're underestimating the amount of cargo that needs to be transferred. There is no way one man can get the job done within the hour."

"Are you saying I'm not a man of my word?"

He folds his arms across his chest in a grumpy way. "I'm saying there is no way you can load the boat with all the cargo in an hour."

My eyes deepen, and my jaw twitches. I hate being underestimated. "Care to make a wager on it?"

He shrugs. *Pussy.*

"If I get it loaded in under an hour, you pay me double," I say. I don't care about the money. I care about putting this motherfucker in his place.

"And if I win?"

"I work for you for a month for free," I say, even though I don't plan on staying that long. I won't lose this bet. I know my capabilities.

The crowd of men around us *oohs* as the wager is placed.

Wayne grins, extending his hand to me. "I love having workers I don't have to pay." His eyes dart over to two of his men that are currently working a year for free. I wouldn't call them workers so much as slaves. They do all the work everyone else doesn't want to do. And not only do they not get paid, they get treated like dirt.

Wayne looks at his watch. "Time starts now."

I shake my head at the dirty bastard as I walk at my normal, casual pace over to the truck. He thinks he's being tricky by starting the time without warning and without me anywhere near the truck, but he's just digging his own grave deeper. The more he messes with me, the more I want to end his life.

I look into the back of the loading truck. There are a dozen crates that usually take two men to lift, and at least fifty bags that need to be carried over. I look in the corner where the dolly is, but one of the wheels has popped off, and the other has a flat.

Bastard.

Guess I'm getting my workout in this morning.

I'll start with the crates first. They are the hardest to move because no matter how strong I am, I can only lift one at a time. Then I can work on the bags which I can transport more quickly.

When I walk out of the truck, carrying one of the crates easily between my arms, I hear the gasps from the men around me.

I snicker. I just wish I could watch Wayne pissing his pants. Julian Reed isn't going to be happy he has to pay me double wages.

Forty-five minutes later, I lift the last five bags, toss them over my shoulder and then start carrying them to the boat.

"Zeke," Julian shouts from his car.

Thank God. I'm tired of dealing with Wayne.

I toss the last of the bags into the boat and then find Wayne's gaze. "You owe me double."

His face goes white in front of his boss.

And then I head over to Julian's car.

Julian glares at Wayne. "He's having you move cargo?"

I nod.

He shakes his head. "Sorry about him, he can't recognize good talent when he sees it."

I shrug. "I think he's just threatened."

He laughs. "Probably."

"You have something better for me to do?"

"Get in," he nods.

I climb into the backseat next to him. And then his driver starts driving as Julian presses the button for the partition to go up.

Julian is dressed in a sharp suit. He looks more like a banker than a drug dealer. I don't understand the appeal of suits. I guess men wear them when they want to look powerful without having to put in the work to gain muscles. Muscles that automatically earn you respect from other men when you walk into the room.

"I think it's time we put your skills to the test," he says.

I nod. I like where this is going. If I can do something big enough to repay the debt I owe him, then I can get off this island. It's beautiful, sure. But it's not home.

Julian saved my life three months ago. He pulled me from the ocean before I nearly drowned. He brought me back to his mansion and flew in the best doctors to take care of me. He said the doctors at the local hospital couldn't have saved me. And after driving by it a few times, I realized he was right. They couldn't have saved my life. I was lucky he did. Julian knew if he saved me, I would owe him. I know he didn't do it out of the goodness of his heart. He saw how large I was and took a chance that I would be able to pay him back in a way worth his time.

"What do you have in mind?" I ask. *Please let it be something that earns me my freedom.* I'm not really his captive. I'm not his slave. But I can't leave in good conscience until I pay him back. It's just the way I am. I've worked for him for two and a half months now. As soon as I healed, I got to work. He insisted on paying me for the work even though I said I would do the work for free. All the time, waiting for a moment when I knew I could finally leave, my conscience clear.

It's taken all of my strength to stay. All I wanted to do was get on the first plane back to Miami. I had friends who depended on me. People I needed to protect. But I knew if I returned in the shape I was in, I would only get them all killed. Just like what happened before. I wasn't as strong as I should have been. And it almost cost me my friends' lives. It almost cost my life. I won't put them in danger again. And I'm afraid if I don't leave here with Julian's good graces that I will be putting them in danger. I will be creating a new enemy.

So that's why I've stayed mute about who I worked for before coming here. At first, I pretended I couldn't even remember my life before. And I sure as hell won't be telling Julian about my boss now. Even though this guy is small fries compared to the great Black empire.

"I have a deal that needs arranging. Wayne hasn't been able to close it for me. And the timing isn't good for me; my biggest client needs my attention. I can't be seen courting another client at the same time. You understand, optics in this business are everything."

"Of course," I say.

"I need someone I can trust. Someone smart to go in my place. Someone who can close the deal. Ensure he chooses me to be his partner. That I'm the one he trusts to manage his shipment. Are you the guy to make that happen?"

He pulls a cigar out of his jacket and lights it. He doesn't offer me one. He knows by now I won't take it. I've been too focused on healing to take pleasure in any sort of vices. My lungs still burn when I breathe from taking in too much saltwater. I can't add smoke inhalation to my list of injuries.

"I can be for the right price."

He laughs. "I assumed you were a good negotiator. Name your price. Want ten percent of the deal?"

I shake my head, my eyes darkening, showing how serious I am. My lips thin, and my shoulders straighten, making me look more powerful. More dangerous. "If I do this, then my debt is clean. I owe you nothing. We are done. You are no longer my boss, and I'm no longer your employee. I've repaid you for saving my life."

Julian's lips twitch. He takes another drag of the cigar and then slowly exhales until the back of the car is filled with smoke.

My lungs ache as I inhale the smoke. My throat itches with the need to cough and remove the fumes. My eyes water, and will be red the rest of the day. But I don't cough, scratch, or cower. I don't show weakness.

Julian wants me to handle a drug deal with a man he is desperate to work with. He's trusting me with this task. I can't show him any weakness. He needs to know that no matter what, I will get the job done.

"Sure. You do the job; you owe me nothing. Although, I hope after you get a taste of working for me, and the money and bonuses that come with it, you will reconsider working for me on a long term basis."

I don't respond. I don't want to lead him on and think that I will work for him. But I don't want to insult him by saying there is no amount of money that could ever make me work for him. My boss is Enzo Black. He's earned that right. He's one of my best friends. I don't want to work for anyone else.

"He's a lucky man," he says.

"Who?"

"Whoever you worked for before I found you. It's obvious you risked your life for him. That you will do anything to return to work for him, even though you've been here for months, and he hasn't even tried to find you."

Because Enzo thinks I'm dead, and he has a woman he loves that he has to protect at all costs.

"I would love to have a man work for me with that kind of loyalty."

You have to earn it. Show that even though you do some bad things, you are fair and honest and do the right thing when it really matters. You will sacrifice your life for mine just as I would mine for yours.

Julian will never be that kind of boss. He likes money and power too much. From what I've seen, he's fair with how he treats his men. He pays them well for the jobs they do, but that's as far as it goes. He's not friends with his men. He doesn't treat them like equals. And he thinks his life is more important than theirs.

"Who is your boss, anyway?" Julian asks, causally taking another puff of his cigar.

But there is nothing casual about his question. He's very curious to know who my boss is. And I don't plan on telling him a damn thing. I'm loyal; I'll protect the Black empire with my life.

"Right now, you."

He chuckles, almost choking on the smoke cloud that surrounds us.

"Good answer." He reaches into his briefcase and pulls out a small stack of papers. "Memorize everything on these, then burn them. We don't leave a paper trail." His eyes focus on mine as I take the papers. He's not sure if I'm anything more than just muscle. He's still not sure I have any brains behind the armor I wear. It's a mistake many men before him have made.

But my brain works just fine. Even after almost drowning and bleeding out in the middle of the fucking ocean.

I'll memorize everything on these papers with no problem. Then I'm going to get Julian this fucking drug deal and get off this fucking island.

But as my eyes skim the papers quickly, I realize Julian isn't the man I thought he is. His soul is darker than I realized. His greed for money has no bounds. And I just walked into his trap.

Because what I'm reading isn't something I would ever do. I've done some bad things in my life. Stolen. Threatened. Beaten. Tortured. Killed. But this is a line I don't cross. I don't traffic humans, and yet that is exactly what Julian is asking me to do.

3

SIREN

WHY DID I end up parked in front of the biggest mansion on the island?

Because I'm stupid.

Because I'm begging to get caught.

Because I like living in danger.

Because I'd rather be trapped in a beautiful cage than continue to live in my own personal hell.

Because I'm desperate.

I consider using the doorbell, but that's really not my style. I don't ask for permission. I never have. I take what is owed to me, even if others disagree. And then I deal with the consequences.

So I walk around to the back of the large all-white building that is just as fake as the man who lives alone inside. The house is three stories tall and the size of a football field. Water weaves through the compound, separating the various buildings from the main house. It looks like an expensive resort, instead of where the devil lives.

I hate this house.

I hate this island.

And I'm finally going to do something about it. A plan forms in my head as I walk to the back door. I'm going to steal something. Something valuable. Something I can easily sell and use to get off this island. Something I can use to start a new life. Something I can use to hide away. Something this man won't even miss.

Who am I kidding?

Julian will realize something is missing from his precious mansion. He lives for his things. He loves the status they give him. He's a little OCD about it. I wouldn't doubt he spends his nights counting all the expensive things in his mansion. They're the only things that can tolerate living in his presence.

I pick the lock on the back door and crack it open, waiting for an alarm to sound. None does.

I've never stolen anything before. That's not the kind of person I am. But I'm desperate. And if anyone deserves to have something stolen, it's Julian Reed.

I step one foot inside, waiting for his army to descend on me. Again, nothing happens.

I grin.

This might actually work.

That, or he'll find me and kill me. Either way, I won't keep living with this pain.

I walk through his house, my hands tempted by all the objects in his house—the paintings, the gold-plated sculptures, the finely threaded fabrics of his furniture. All are too big for me to take. I need something small. Something that can easily be sold.

Jewelry, I decide.

I head up the staircase in search of his bedroom. I'm sure he keeps some jewelry up there.

I haven't seen any sign that he is home. But Julian doesn't scare me. He's a fucking drug dealer who thinks he's a bigger deal than he is. He's a nothing—a boy playing with his daddy's money.

And if he catches me, I'll offer to suck his dick or something to get out. He's a good looking man, even if he is evil.

I find his bedroom. It's dark, and the door is closed. I lean my ear against his door—nothing.

I open the door. It creaks, but no one comes for me. No one knows I'm here.

I step inside. I consider turning the lights on but decide I've tested fate enough. However, I'm not good at seeing in the dark, no matter how much my eyes try to adjust. I don't make a good criminal. I'm just hungry and desperate enough to try anything.

My hand finds the wall, and I walk with my hand against it until I reach an opening—the bathroom.

My hand trails over the counter as I search for a jewelry box, anything that contains something expensive that can be easily sold, but not easily missed.

Jackpot.

I find a box sitting out in plain sight on the middle of the counter. I flip it open and dig to the bottom, hoping to find something that will change my life.

I pull out a bracelet, dripping in diamonds.

I grin—this would give me a new life.

I go to put the bracelet into my pocket, when a hand grabs me out of the darkness.

I close my eyes, hoping this is all a dream, a figment of my imagination, my worst nightmare. That when I open my eyes, I'll be in my bed, not here, stealing from the most dangerous man on the island.

But when I open them, I'm still in the darkness. And Julian is still gripping my hand.

"What are you doing?" he asks, his voice curious more than angry.

Think, quickly! I can find a way out of this.

I stare at the bracelet.

"I'm—" Fuck, I can't answer.

"Are you the new maid?" he whispers into my neck. He releases my wrist, but his heavy breath has me captured. His body is pressed against my ass and back, and he sweeps my air off my neck so he can own that part of me too.

I breathe out with a shaky breath, but can't force my lips to say *yes.*

"Is there a reason you are cleaning in the dark?"

The power is out.

I couldn't find the light switch.

I prefer the dark.

So many lies fill my head. But none of them can flow through my lips.

"I'm not the maid. I came here to steal something of value I could use to get off this fucking island. Something you wouldn't miss. Something I could use to start a new life." *Something to heal my pain and fix my problems.*

The lights flick on in that moment, and I'm exposed. The lights shouldn't make a difference, but they do. In the dark, I could have spilled all of my secrets but in the light...I want to close up every thought I have and hide them away from this man.

Julian Reed is well-known on the island. I've served him in bars where I worked as a bartender numerous times. But seeing him now, pressed against me, the first two buttons of his shirt undone, his hair slicked back, and his eyes focused on me and not some business deal he's working on, I realize how intimidating a man he is.

"What's your name?" he asks.

Lie.

Don't tell him the truth. Keep all of your secrets.

I can't lie, but I refuse to answer.

His eyes light up when he realizes this.

"You can't lie, can you?"

"No...I can't."

He shakes his head as he brushes more of my hair off my neck, fascinated by me.

I'm silent. *I can't lie.* Every time I try, my body or words betray me. *Even if it could have saved me now.* If I had just pretended to be the maid like he guessed, I would be safe.

"What's your deal, pet?"

"Pet?"

He grins as he puts his hands in his pockets as if trying to make me more comfortable by preventing himself from touching me. I'm not falling for it. I know this man will hurt me before the night is over. He'll rape me. Torture me. Kill me. Him putting his hands in his pockets doesn't make him any less of a threat to me. I turn to face him.

"Yes, you are now my pet. Unless you tell me your name, and I like it better than 'pet.' Then I might call you by your name instead."

My lips beg me to lie. To tell him any name. I don't want him to know who I am, but I don't want him to call me pet.

He cracks his neck back and forth casually, waiting for me to answer.

"You're an intriguing creature, pet."

My eyes burn red.

He laughs, and then one of his hands reaches out automatically.

"I'm going to enjoy you so much, pet."

"No," I whisper, trying to step back as his hand strokes my face, but there is nowhere for me to go. I'm trapped between him and the counter at my back.

I turn my head, trying to be as defiant as I can.

"I'm sorry. I shouldn't have broken into your house and tried to steal from you. Let me go. I'll owe you. I'll work for you for free."

He tilts his head, studying me. "Will you now?"

I nod, hoping to god he needs free labor more than he wants to do bad things to me.

"I don't think you really have a say in the matter, pet. You broke into my house. You stole from me. Now you have to pay the consequences."

"Are you going to call the police?"

He laughs. "No, pet. I'm not going to call the police."

"What do you want from me then?"

"I want your fiery spirit."

His eyes heat over my body.

"I want your perfect lips that can't spill a lie."

I gasp as his thumb traces over my bottom lip.

"I want to own your desperation."

He spins me around, and then I'm facing the mirror again. His hand is on my throat and hip. And I'm pulled tight to his rough body.

I can't breathe, but not because of how he is holding me. Because I'm waiting for the rest of his words to fall. I'm waiting to hear what my fate is.

"I want to harness you. I want to teach you how to use your assets to my advantage. I want to own your body. I want to control your mind."

I'm never breathing again. Maybe if I stop breathing, I won't live long enough for any of his words to come true.

"And what if I don't do what you want?" I ask, with words bolder than I'm feeling.

"Oh, pet. I always get what I want."

4

ZEKE

THERE HAS to be a different way I can repay Julian.

That sentence has played in my head over and over and over. Every day of the last week, I've tried to come up with a different plan—a different way to pay him back.

He saved my life. *I could save his.*

But he never puts himself in any danger. I've never seen a leader of a criminal organization keep his hands as clean as he does. Instead of doing the dirty work himself, he always has his employees do anything remotely risky. And the few times he has to take meetings in person, he does it in his mansion, where I know he has plenty of security features.

My old boss was in the security business. I know security when I see it, even though his is well hidden. I can spot the cameras, the infrared, the panic buttons. I can spot the bulletproof walls.

Julian knows he has enemies. He knows he is exposed if he puts himself out there. So he hides. People know who he is, but he rarely shows himself in public. Somehow, that makes him even more powerful.

But it makes it very difficult for me to be able to save his life to pay him back.

I'm stuck in the horrible position of getting him a partnership with a man who traffics humans. And I don't see a way out.

I could run away. Not repay my debt.

But Julian's not the kind of man who lets a debt go. He would come for me. And in turn, he'd come for my boss. He'd come for the Black empire I'm desperate to protect.

No way will I let that happen.

But I really don't want a permanent mark on my soul.

I step out of my beat-up truck and look up at the enormous warehouse sitting on the edge of the island. It doesn't look like anything special. Just four walls with a tin roof. It looks like any other storage facility. But this one has one main difference. Instead of storing merchandise or supplies, this building stores people like animals.

"Ah, you must be Mr. Zeke," a man says as soon as I step out of the car.

He's dressed in a sharp-looking suit just like Julian. But unlike Julian, this man has a gut that sticks out, defeating the purpose of the suit. He looks weak, not powerful.

"It's just Zeke. You must be Oscar," I say as I walk to him and force myself to extend my hand.

He takes my hand and shakes it. And I can't resist squeezing his hand a little too harshly.

He just grins at my forceful handshake.

"Mr. Reed has said many good things about you. He said you were his best up and coming man. That you could easily be his number two."

I nod. "I'm the best at my job." My stomach churns bile into my throat. I'm good enough to actually do this job; to convince this man that he should work with Julian and me. I have the skills to ensure shipments happen swiftly and accurately.

"Come, come. Let me show you around, and then we can talk business," Oscar says, extending his hand to lead me toward the building I want to empty and burn to the ground.

I don't smile, as opposed to the petite man as he leads me into the building, showing me around the building like he's giving me a tour of the Louvre instead of where humanity comes to die. Good thing I almost never smile. Frowning feeds into my scary appearance. It makes me look more menacing.

Fuck, how did my life lead me here?

I've seen a lot of sinful shit in my life. I've seen more men killed in front of me, by me, than I ever thought I would. I've tortured people. Watched the life leave their eyes. I've known women who were raped. But nothing in my life could prepare me for what I saw when I entered this building.

I could feel the fear, pain, and anger the second I entered the building. I have an uncanny ability to feel emotions emanating from nearby people. I don't understand it. I can sense things others are feeling. I haven't even seen another person so far on our tour, but I've never felt so much pain in one place before.

"This way," Oscar says excitedly.

I glare as I follow the pudgy little man.

He opens the door, and I step through to a room I wasn't expecting to see.

"What's this?" I ask.

He grins like he's about to show off the Sistine Chapel instead of his demonic headquarters. "This is where we hold our main event. We only hold an event here twice a year for our biggest clients who spend the most money. It's an auction of sorts. We parade our best women in front of them, and the highest bidder wins the prize."

A low growl escapes me as he speaks about selling women, but the asshole is too busy to notice as he gloats about how he turned this part of the warehouse into a fancy showroom filled with tables, bars, and a stage that shows off the women's best assets.

"Why don't you hold more frequent events here? That way, you wouldn't need us to transport and sell your remaining women for you. You would get all the money yourself," I say, hoping this man is just an idiot, and once I point out the obvious, he will have no need for us. Sure, I'll fail the task Julian gave me. But maybe he'll let me try again with a shipment of drugs or weapons, anything but people.

He sighs. "It would make business a lot easier. But it's just not feasible. The richest people in the world come here for the event. It's our biggest money earning night of the year. But we hide it under the guise of the weekend-long yachting event. That's how we keep suspicions low. The men all stay at the Four Seasons, the luxury hotel where the event is held. They all attend, and then we sneak them here under the darkness of the night. Our little island would get too much press and attention if the richest in the world were all flying here on a monthly basis on the same weekend."

I frown. "But this island is beautiful with plenty of luxury hotels. Why couldn't you just house the women here, and when one of the buyers comes, bring them here individually to have their pick?"

"It's too expensive to feed the whores while we wait for the men to come to us. And even though this is one of our most profitable nights, not all of the men can travel to us.

Sometimes we need to go to them. Which is why we hire out. You take on all the risk, while we get all the reward."

Tell me about it.

"So then why would we want to do business with you if we take on all the risk?" I ask.

He raises his eyebrow. "Because we aren't the only ones who get a reward. If we strike a deal, then we split profits fifty-fifty. And the amount of money we pay is bigger than the petty little drugs and weapons Mr. Reed currently moves. This would put him on a whole new level. Supposedly, Mr. Reed is the best at transporting things while flying under the radar."

"He is," I agree.

"Well, that's why you are here. To prove to me you can handle the job, not question why I run my business the way I do."

"No, I'm not here to convince you of anything. You know of Julian's reputation. You can see I mean business."

He laughs. "I don't believe anyone who shows up in ripped jeans and a man bun is serious about doing business with me. And I don't think anyone who calls his boss by his first name respects him."

I snarl, this time, he hears it. He freezes.

"I'm here to see if we can strike a deal. But I won't let my boss enter a relationship with a man who is an inadequate business partner. I'm doing my due diligence.

"And if you don't already think we are a good partnership for you, then you are an idiot. You didn't choose our island for the scenery. You chose our island because of Julian. You knew he was the best at transportation. You need him; he doesn't need you. He will be just fine without your business. And I respect Julian greatly. And he respects me, which is why we are on a first-name basis."

Oscar's eyes dart side-to-side as he takes me in—how fucking serious I am.

"Then he sent the right man. Because I don't do business with desperate men, and that's exactly what I thought Mr. Reed was when he called trying to get my business. You just changed my mind." He turns to continue the tour.

"We want sixty."

He pauses, his head swiveling to look at me.

"You heard me. We want sixty percent. And we want half of it upfront."

He narrows his eyes. "The deal was for fifty-fifty. That's my final offer. It's the arrangement I have with all of my partners. I capture the women and hold them for no more than a week. Then you arrange deals with buyers and transport them. It's a fifty-fifty arrangement."

"No, it's not. Finding sellers, vetting them, and then transporting the women takes a lot longer than grabbing them and holding them here for a week. We could have to hold onto the women for weeks, months even. We take on the risk of selling and transporting them to a client who could be working for the cops, while you sit back here protected from everyone.

"If we get caught, we go to jail. We lose everything. While you just lose your partner. We want a bigger cut— sixty," I say, hoping this will ensure we don't have a deal. If I push him hard enough, he will back down and say that he won't do business with us. And if Julian asks, I can tell him I didn't think it was a good deal because we deserved a bigger cut. And I'll personally find him a deal that will make up for the lost income—one selling drugs, not people.

"You better be worth it, Zeke," he says with a frown.

Dammit.

"Come on, let me show you where we store the women.

Then I can see if we have a suit that fits you. You aren't showing up for the biggest night of the year dressed like a bum."

I frown. I'm not wearing a fucking suit. That is not my style. And I'm tall and bulky enough to know there is no way he will find a suit big enough to fit me.

I follow Oscar behind the stage, trying to prepare myself. But nothing could prepare me to see women in chains. And not the kinky, consenting kind. The kind no woman has the strength to break free from.

I prepare myself to hear begging, to see tears, but these women don't look at me as their savior. They think I'm just like Oscar. They think I'm a villain that one of them will eventually be sold to. They don't know I would never buy any of them. If I could, I would set them all free.

Instead, I look at hollow eyes, tight lips, and women trying to hide their bodies from my view.

"They are bewitching, aren't they?" Oscar says, grabbing one of the women by the chin and lifting her face up to examine her like an animal.

I tense, but don't react. *How can this be real? How can people be this cruel?*

"We already have a transporter for this group. But we will have over a hundred women for you in a few weeks."

A hundred women—fuck.

"And then we will have a new shipment for you in three weeks after that if the first deal works out. So I suggest you move quickly."

We will get another hundred women in less than a month—fuck, fuck, fuck.

We walk further down the hallway to where there is a large cage filled with twenty women. Each of them is shackled at their arms and legs as if they would have the strength to get through the metal bars holding them in.

"These are the women for tonight. The most beautiful, attractive high priced women we could find. Some are virgins; some are women from high-class families. All will go for more than a million a piece."

Jesus Christ.

"But if Mr. Reed wants first pick, of course, that can be arranged for the right price. Take a look," Oscar says.

I'm sick. I'm seconds away from puking up everything I've ever eaten. My face turns green, but I'm not going to let Oscar know that. I don't have a plan. Not yet, but I will.

I look over the women with a deep scowl, knowing I can't save them. I can't protect them.

I glance at the last woman, and my heart stops. I squat down in front of her, getting a better look at this exquisite creature.

The most alluring eyes look back at me. This woman isn't scared. She's full of fight. I see the wheels in her brain turning, determined to find a way out of this situation. She's not going to go down without fighting.

But she's going to lose. I know the amount of security Oscar has. I can't save her. If I find her leaving, I will be forced to capture her and turn her back in. She needs to accept this is her new life. It will be easier for her.

But the fight in her eyes, long gone in the others, isn't the only thing that makes me pause looking at her. There is something else about her. Something that has my brain spinning, trying its best to remember why I know her. A wash of déjà vu crashes through me when I look at her.

"Aww, this one is going to go for the highest price tonight, guaranteed. She's beautiful and a fighter. The others are already broken. She's going to make me a lot of money. I'd guess three million. The men prefer a fighter. They want to be the one to break a woman. And she is begging to be broken."

"Where did you find her?"

"This one washed ashore during the last storm. The ocean finally gave us a gift for once."

The ocean.

Julian didn't pull me from the ocean.

This angel did.

Siren—that was her name.

I still owe Julian for getting me medical attention, but I don't owe him as much as I first thought. Because Siren was the one who pulled me from the ocean. She stopped me from drowning. She put her hands over my wounds to keep me from bleeding out. She sang to me to keep me calm. She dragged my lifeless body to her car. She brought me to the only person on the island with the money and power to save me.

And what did the world give her for saving me? Imprisonment and the verge of being sold into sexual slavery.

She glares at me. She remembers me. And she hates me. She blames me for her predicament. And she thinks she saved a monster. She thinks I'm just like the men who took her.

I stand up. "How long until the event?"

"Three hours."

I nod. "We better get ready then."

"Excellent." Oscar starts gabbing about everything still to be done. I barely listen, though. All I can think about is Siren. About how she saved my life. And now, I have to save hers.

5

———

SIREN

I HATE SILENCE. But I hate the sound of sniffling even more. It's like someone is stabbing my ears with knives. That's the reaction I feel every time I hear a sniffle, a cough, a muffled cry. Not because I care or have a heart for the other women who are captured with me. I do, of course, have a heart. I want them all to find their way out of this mess the same as me. But right now, I can't think about escaping because my brain is consumed with sniffle, drip, sniffle, cough.

Fuck, I grab my ears with my hands trying to get the sounds to stop, trying to get the anxiety building in my chest to dissipate. But it only grows. There is a name for my condition—misophonia. It means normal, ordinary sounds cause a visceral reaction in my body. Usually, I can avoid the sounds. If someone is slurping too loudly at a coffee shop, I can leave. If my friend is chewing too loudly at dinner, I can talk over the noise. If someone is sneezing on the bus, I can play music louder in my earbuds.

But I can't do any of those things right now. I'm stuck in a cage with a dozen terrified women. A hundred more are tied up nearby. All of them releasing a cacophony of various

47

noises in the otherwise silent room. No one dares to talk, too afraid they will become the first victim to be beaten, raped, or sold.

None of them understand it doesn't matter if we are the first or the last; we all face the same fate. We are all about to be sold like cattle. We have all lost our dignity, our human right to freedom. We are now property.

Deep breath in and then out, I practice my calming technique, and I feel the anxiety lower an inch from my throat to my chest. Most people think anxiety is all in your head; it isn't. It takes over everything in your body. Your stomach aches, your chest pounds unable to catch a breath, your throat closes up, your mouth runs dry, and even your bones throb from the anxiety. Relieving a single one of those pains is a success in my book.

"What do you think is going to happen?" the woman to my right whispers into my ear. She's dressed in a gray suit, with a white blouse underneath. Her blouse is now covered in dirt, her mascara is running down her face, and her hair looks like it hasn't been washed in a week. I would guess a week ago she was a high-powered lawyer or businesswoman —now she's nothing but tears. But she is strong enough to ask me a question in the silence even though there are guards watching us. I admire her bravery.

"They are going to sell us," I say flatly, not sugarcoating our outcome.

The woman grips her neck, as if she can't believe her fate.

"For what purpose?" her voice is weaker now.

I blink rapidly, looking at her. *She can't be serious?* Does she not realize there is only one reason to sell another human being? *Money.* These men want money. And the men who are buying us want power. They want to control us, live out their sick fantasies, rape us, torture us, and, the kind ones, kill us.

But I see her trembling hand; I see the tears welling up in her eyes, the way she bites her bottom lip. She's about to break out into an uncontrollable sob. That's a sound that will rip right through my body and bring back every drop of anxiety I was feeling.

"What's your name?" I ask.

"Alice."

She doesn't ask for mine. She's too focused on her own fate to see that she isn't the only woman who is about to face the same outcome.

"Okay, Alice. Are you married?"

She shakes her head.

"Have a boyfriend?"

Again she shakes her head no.

"Kids?"

No—she was probably too focused on her work to date. She seems like a smart, ambitious, gorgeous woman in her late twenties. She probably never bothered to date. Now, I'm sure she wishes she did. Then maybe she'd have that love to focus on. That strength to pull her through this. That hope that her man would come and save her. That fairytale that love conquers all, that it ultimately wins.

I laugh.

"What's so funny?" She asks.

"Sorry," I say, thinking about how love only makes you weaker, not stronger. By not falling in love, this woman proved her ultimate superpower. She is strong enough to handle anything on her own.

I grip her shoulders and look her straight in the eyes. "Alice, you are strong. You have not only survived these last twenty plus years without a man, but you have thrived. You have become a fierce, badass woman. No matter what happens, you lived a great life. And you are strong enough to handle whatever is coming your way. Remember that."

My words are meant to be a pep talk, but it seems to have the opposite effect on Alice, who bursts into tears. A domino effect of emotional distress rips through the group until the entire room is crying, sniffling, sucking in tears—all the things I hate.

Dammit.

Sighing, I bring my knees up to my chest and my long brown hair around my ears, trying my best to tune them all out.

"Stop that racket, you stupid whores!" a guard yells, pounding his gun against the bars.

The room instantly falls silent, and I find myself liking the guard a bit more for making the room go silent again. *How fucked up is that?*

Our cell door is opened, and three guards enter the small cage holding me and eleven other women. We are all handcuffed at the hands and feet, but I don't think the cuffs are needed for most of the women. They are all too terrified to run or fight. They've already accepted their fate.

The guards start grabbing women up off the floor until they are on their shaky feet. I refuse to be pulled up by my hair or arms, so I stand before a guard can get to me. I will not be afraid—I refuse. As long as I don't say that I'm scared, I won't be. I can't lie to myself and say that I'm happy or unafraid. Deep down there is some fear, but as long as I can't focus on it, then I'm not lying or telling the truth. I'm just focusing on other things.

A guard reaches me, seeing me standing eye to eye to him. I'm tall, even without heels.

"Are you going to be a problem?" he asks, eyeing me before uncuffing my ankles.

I raise an eyebrow. "Only if you try to hurt me."

He huffs and then grabs my arm roughly. I fight, trying to pull my arm free as I kick at his legs.

He shakes me; I fight harder.

He stops, I stop.

He sighs. "Fine, we will do this your way. I've dealt with your type before, and I'd like to have children someday."

I grin when he releases my arm. I'm the only woman left in the room. He correctly guessed that I would kick him in the balls if he manhandled me too much.

"This way," he points to the exit of the cage.

I start walking untouched.

He verbally commands me to walk down the hallway to a small room where three women wait for me.

I spot a chair in the center that's meant to glamorize me—make me look like a woman again instead of a gaunt invalid that hasn't been fed in a week.

"Sit," the man says.

I sit, knowing he is the least of my worries.

"I'll be right outside the door. Don't give them any trouble, or I'll break your wrist."

"You can't do that. I doubt the men who are waiting for us want to buy broken women."

He frowns. "That's why I said wrist instead of foot or nose. The men won't be able to tell your wrist is broken. The swelling won't happen until after you've already been sold, and by then, we can just say they were the ones who broke it."

With that, he walks out, slamming the door.

The three women all put their heads down, none of

them looking me in the eyes as they begin to work on my hair, face, and nails.

"Why do you work for these men?" I ask.

None of them answer me.

Two of the women murmur something low and quiet to each other. It's then that I realize they don't speak English. Two of the women look Hispanic. One of the women is black and doesn't chat with the other two. I look like a mix of the three women.

My skin is tan in an exotic way. I don't know the nationality of my birth parents, but I would guess I'm a mix of several ethnicities. My adoptive parents always treated me as if I were a bad person for having an unknown origin. My culture is a strength—I am a mix of everything and hence know more of the world because of it.

The women chat again.

"Why do you work for these men?" I ask in Spanish.

All of the women freeze but don't answer me. They heard and understood what I said, though.

So I try again. "Help me. Or at least help them," I say in Spanish.

Nothing.

One woman files my fingers harder until I'm not sure I'll have a fingernail left.

I sigh.

"They won't answer you," the third woman says.

"Why not?" I ask, looking into her eyes. She meets my gaze, and I realize she's old enough to be my grandmother. The other two women are closer to my age.

"Because they are afraid. Everyone is afraid. They risk facing the same fate as you if they help you."

I look at the two beautiful women working on my hair

and nails. They aren't wearing any makeup, they wear their hair back in buns, trying to hide their beauty.

"The only reason they aren't sold is that they can do hair and makeup."

I nod. "And you? Will you help?"

The older woman grabs my hand and places it between her two hands, trying to comfort me. It works, my insides warm a little at the touch.

"Do I look like I'm strong enough to be able to help you escape?"

I sigh.

"I can't help you or any of the other women escape. But I can offer you words."

I nod for her to speak, even though I don't think words are going to be able to help me right now.

"Give them hell."

Three little words—*give them hell.*

I scrunch my nose, and she laughs.

"I see how much fighting spirit you have inside you—use it. The ones who last—the ones who make the men fall in love with them are the ones who eventually gain control. They become the masters.

"You have what it takes. You will not only survive, but you will become powerful. You will rule. You will have the ability to one day put an end to this. So give them hell."

Give them hell.

I nod. *That, I can do.*

She smiles at my reaction and then gets back to work at plucking my eyebrows.

The rest of my time with the women is silent as they work. They paint my nails, curl my mud-brown hair, decorate my face in makeup, and wax off every piece of body hair. Then they leave me alone with a rack of lingerie and a robe.

They didn't have to tell me what to do, I already know. Pick out the piece of lingerie to wear on stage.

I don't want to wear any lingerie.

But the guard's words haunt me. If I go for more money, I will be better taken care of. I'll be more valuable. So I need to choose what I wear carefully.

I look over the garments. Most are white—innocent.

I laugh, I'm not innocent. I'm not an angel. Those were the words I said to Zeke. *I'm not an angel.* But neither is he—the bastard. I saved his life, and he repaid that debt by being an even bigger schmuck than I thought possible.

Fuck him.

Fuck them all.

Give them hell.

I grin when I find the last garment on the end of the rack. I put it on and stare at myself in the mirror before I put the robe on, covering my body.

Just as I finish veiling myself with the robe, the guard opens the door without knocking.

"Time to go back to your cage," he says.

I stand taller than him now in my heels, and the lustful look on his face as he takes in my appearance tells me that even with the robe on, I would go for a lot of money. But once I take the robe off, my price will skyrocket.

He clears his throat and holds the door open for me. I brush past him as I strut.

And I hear him curse under his breath. I smirk, feeling powerful.

He may not be able or willing to save me. But someday, I'm going to find a man who can—a man who is willing to risk everything for me. Then I will have all the power.

I walk back to the cage where the other eleven women sit. This time, none of us are handcuffed. We are all wearing robes covering the intimate pieces of our bodies that will eventually be exposed. Every woman's hair is styled, her face painted. Each looks a little different. Some look like innocent angels; the youngest woman even has pigtails to make her look younger. A couple of the women have dark red lips to make them look older and more mature. But all of the women look more terrified instead of determined.

The apparent man in charge enters the cage with two of the guards. One of the guards has a notebook and pen in his hand. The boss takes his time walking around the cage, studying each of us like he's trying to determine how much we should go for.

I want to stick my foot out and try to trip him, but I resist the urge as he starts pointing to women and assigning each a random number. I realize he's deciding the order in which we will be trotted out on stage. He's starting with the women he thinks will go for the least and ending on the most expensive.

He hasn't pointed to me yet. Maybe because he's forgotten I exist as he walks around the circle.

I swear my foot sticks out on its own accord. Next thing I know, he stumbles over the heel of my foot.

I pull it back to my body quickly. I'm afraid, but knowing if I'm punished, it will be minimal. They don't want to damage me right before the show.

The man squats down in front of me, looking me in the eye. I think he's going to yell at me. Punch me. Make me feel some pain for tripping him.

Instead, he grins crookedly, a toothpick sliding out between his yellow teeth.

"Twenty," he says, looking at me. "She will easily go for

five mill. Maybe more, she has a fight to her the men can't resist. They will all want to be the one to break her."

Five million dollars, holy hell.

Maybe the advice the woman gave me was bad? If I give them too much hell, then they will want to break me.

The man walks out and through a door to what I realize is a stage.

I can hear the sound of music playing in the next room. The show is about to start. And I can practically feel every heart in the room speed up at the sound.

A few minutes later, one of the guards is dragging out the woman labeled number one. She's one of the youngest. I would guess seventeen or eighteen. She's still a baby in many ways. And she's about to be thrust on stage and sold.

The guard pushes her out and leaves the door to the stage open so we can all see to the stage. I don't know if it's meant to intimidate or encourage us to be able to see how the previous women are treated. But the first woman stands in the middle of the stage, gripping her robe nervously as men yell out numbers in the crowd.

After a few minutes of her being on stage, the man in charge asks her to disrobe. But she only grips it tighter.

He snaps his fingers, and two of the guards rip the robe from her body. She crumbles to the floor in tears, trying her best to cover her almost naked body.

All of the women in the cage turn away, looking away from her humiliation.

One by one, each woman is dragged to the stage and faces the same fate. Most sell for between one and three million. Each is forced to disrobe. Each is humiliated and frightened beyond possibility.

But I won't be. *Give. Them. Hell.*

I plan to.

The guards outside the cage start drinking, enjoying the fun and amount of money their boss is making, which will obviously trickle down to them.

And then I'm the only woman left in the cage.

My heart speeds uncontrollably as I prepare for my turn. I'm not sure what I'm going to do, but I won't cower. I won't let them have my power.

Finally, the man who has been my guard walks to the entrance of the cage. He motions for me as I stand.

"Your turn." His eyes light as he says it, as if he wishes he had enough money to bid on me.

"Give me a shot of tequila."

"What? No."

"I'll go for more than double any other woman here if you give me a shot. You can tell your boss it was because of the shot of liquid courage that helped me to perform. You will have gotten your boss more money and maybe a new strategy to help future women."

He frowns but hands me a shot glass. He grabs a bottle as all eyes of the other guards focus in on us. He pours the tequila into the shot glass and fills it to the rim.

"You owe me, and don't worry. I plan to collect on my debt," he says, threatening me.

But I won't be threatened. He can't hurt me. No man can. I know what it's like to be betrayed by a man. And the only way a man can hurt me anymore is if I give them my heart—something I will never do again.

I throw the shot back into my mouth.

I feel the warm liquid trickle down my throat and warm my stomach.

It's my last moment of happiness, the last moment that is truly mine before I walk on the stage.

I hand the shot glass back to my guard, and then I strut

up the stairs to the stage. I'll give them hell alright. The men will wish they never captured me.

Because I'm about to tap into my power tonight. I may not win the fight, but by the time I'm through with them, I will drain them all of their power.

Even if it's the last thing I do.

6

―――――

ZEKE

This is my nightmare.

Men are sitting at small circular tables scattered throughout a dark floor. Each table can sit three men max, but only a couple are filled. Most men are sitting by themselves with a phone in one hand, a drink in the other, and cigar puffing out of their mouths.

Each man is assigned a scantily dressed waitress to do more than just serve drinks. They are here to tease the men before the show, so maybe they will open their bank accounts wider.

"What can I get you, sugar?" The waitress assigned to me asks.

"I'm good," I say, lifting my barely drank scotch.

She gives me a knowing look as she eyes the scotch.

"Got a weak stomach, sugar?"

I growl—she's just trying to goad me into drinking more so I'll be more hasty with my money. But I need my wits about me tonight.

A man at the table over must hear our conversation because he starts murmuring to the man on his right.

Great, I'm going to be known as a pussy.

Fuck—I can't let that happen.

Not because I care what people think of me, but I can't draw any suspicions. I need Julian to think I'm an equal to him. And if Oscar thinks of me as a pussy, then he'll tell Julian.

I down the expensive scotch.

"Another," I say.

She picks up the glass, her eyes brightening, and her hips swaying as she walks away from me to retrieve another drink.

The lights dim even more, until the only lights left in the room are the single candles on each table.

Oscar walks out onto the stage as a spotlight follows him.

"Welcome, friends. I have quite a show for you."

Some of the men applaud and hoop excitedly, while others stare at their phones like they couldn't be more bored.

I do neither. I reach for where my drink once sat and find the table empty. I need my damn waitress to get back with my glass, so I have something to squeeze to death while I try to think of a plan.

"The first beautiful woman I have for you is more girl than woman. Let's hear it for Chaste."

The light flickers to stage right as a young blonde woman is pushed onto the stage by two guards. She stumbles, falling to the ground as she grips the thin white robe around her body. She doesn't realize the robe is practically see-through in the bright stage light. We can already see her body. A body that looks barely older than fifteen.

Jesus Christ. I glance around at the men. They are sick.

Not only are they selling women, but they are selling underage women.

The waitress finally returns with my drink, and I down it. I'm going to need a lot of alcohol to get through tonight.

"Keep them coming," I growl at her as I crush the glass in my hand, not caring who sees.

"Of course, sugar." She brushes her hand over my shoulder in a seductive way before she walks away. But the most attractive woman in the world could strip naked in front of me and offer to suck my dick, and I wouldn't get turned on right now. I'm beyond pissed that men are this disgusting.

Oscar starts the bidding at half a million.

That number quickly shoots up to over two million for the young virgin.

But Oscar isn't satisfied. He snaps his fingers, and the guards return to the stage. Her rope is ripped from her body until she is standing in white lingerie, revealing small breasts, a flat stomach, and bony hips. She's so young. Untouched. And scared to death.

I skim the crowd trying to memorize every face of the men who are bidding on her—reserving a special place in my memory filled with the torturous thoughts of what I'm going to do to them when I'm finally a free man who can come after them.

The woman sells for $2.5 million.

And seconds later, another woman is dragged onto the stage to do the whole show all over again. This one is slightly older than the first, but just barely. She wears the same face of terror as the girl before her.

My stomach contracts tightly at the sight. I could easily vomit I'm so angry and disgusted. Instead, I sip on the drink my waitress brought me.

"Young women aren't your thing? Don't worry, they always save the more mature women for the end. You would think the young ones would be the most popular, but they aren't. The young ones the men can get all the time.

"Just flash some money in a twenty-something's face, and she will do anything for you. It's the older women—the ones who have a career, a husband, kids, a life. The smart ones are hard to get. They aren't as easily broken as the young ones." She sighs. "Around number fifteen is when I expect you to start bidding, stud."

And then she's gone. I'm not going to bid. If I do, it will be just so it's not obvious that I'm a traitor. But I won't win a woman.

I'm here to protect.

That's what I do—protect people. But I can't protect any of these women. Not without getting a lot of them killed, myself included. I just came back from the dead; I don't want to return so quickly. I would risk it if I had a real shot at getting them to safety, but I don't. I don't have a big enough truck to transport all of them in. I don't have a boat to help them escape. I would just be leading them all to their deaths.

They might prefer it to where they are going, but I can't be responsible for getting them killed.

Another woman appears on stage, gripping the robe like it's her only lifeline. The only thing keeping her safe.

Is it..?

The woman finally looks up into the crowd of dark faces.

No, it's not Siren.

But the next woman could be.

What the hell am I going to do?

I can't let her be sold. I can't let her become a sex slave. She saved my life; I owe this to her. It's as if fate stepped in and is requiring me to save her life. I'm in the right place at the right time to protect her. Just like she was in the right place at the right time to save me.

But how do I save a woman currently being held by my boss' client?

I could kidnap her.

Take her at gunpoint.

Or sneak her out before she was transferred to her new owner.

I could get a boat or a plane out of here. Take her anywhere in the world.

But Julian would know. He has enough resources to come after us both. We would always be running. She would never really be safe.

And I could never return to my life before. I would never bring them into more danger.

Besides, I'm not sure if I could rescue her without us being caught. There are cameras, guards, and locked doors between us and a chance at freedom. I might not even get her out the door.

More women are brought on stage, each more terrified than the one before. The girls being shown now are women, not girls—most in their late twenties to early thirties. Some even have a tan line where a wedding ring used to rest.

Only two women left—one is Siren.

I hold my breath as the second to last woman is pushed out onto the stage.

Blonde.

Not Siren.

Fuck.

Only one woman left. And then the show will be over. My time is up. I need a plan—now.

I don't listen to the bids. I can't focus on anything except the anxiety in my chest as I wait for Siren.

The room falls silent again, as the woman is dragged off the stage.

"We saved the best for last. This woman is exotic, beauty itself. She has a mane of hair. Red fuck me lips. Eyes like fire. Flawless skin. And tits for days."

The room cheers in anticipation of the last woman. There are only twenty women to be sold and thirty men to buy them. It ensures that the last woman goes for the most. Not all men will leave with a woman, at least not a woman from the select group. I'm sure they can go backstage and have their pick of the rest before they are shipped out.

But they don't get the honor of having one of the "best."

I wait for the familiar push and stumble of Siren onto the stage. But it doesn't come.

Instead, *click, click, click.*

The room is silent except for the click of her heels against the hard wood of the stairs.

The entire room takes a deep breath as she appears on stage. And the oxygen in my lungs vanishes entirely.

Siren doesn't get pushed into the center like any of the other women. She struts, owning the stage like it was her idea in the first place.

There is no fear in her eyes, just anger.

She flips her long tresses of brown hair from one shoulder to the other so her eyes can shoot daggers in each man's direction. Her lips purse tightly, prepared to bite us all for putting her in this situation.

And the robe barely covers her body with a simple tie; she doesn't bother to grip it tightly like the other women.

The room is still silent, glued to the goddess in front of us as she takes center stage.

What is she doing? Does she think if she seems willing she won't be sold to such a monster?

But then her face turns wicked. Her eyes shine with the fiercest fire. And her middle finger flips us all the bird.

I laugh at the fierceness exuding from her.

"Fuck you all," she says.

I bite my bottom lip, more entranced with this woman than I've ever been before.

Hoops and hollers and whistles from the men around me tell me I'm not the only one infatuated with her—she has the entire room under her spell. I don't doubt if she started ordering men around, they would do as she asked. Several of the men are clearly submissives, looking for a strong woman to tell them what to do.

But those aren't the men that scare me. It's the other men. The men who haven't bid on a single woman yet. Who have lifted their gaze from their phones to look at her now. And they are looking at her like they want to devour her. Like they can't wait to break her. They see her as a game they plan on winning.

"I told you I saved the best for last. Who wants to start the bidding on our wild stallion here?" Oscar says.

"I'm not a fucking stallion. I'm a woman!" Siren shouts at him.

He just grins—loving her performance, knowing it's going to get him more money.

I smell sex and money in the air—a battle is about to happen.

I tear my gaze from Siren to look at the men who are pining to win her. So many fucking erections fill the darkened room.

Fucking disgusting.

I close my eyes, trying to break the image from my head.

I take a sip of the scotch, washing the repugnant feeling down.

And then I open my eyes, looking up at Siren, who is now stripping out of her robe and throwing it angrily into the crowd.

She's not dressed as an angel, like most of the women. Or black like the last third. She's in a red, fiery number. One that matches her red lips, but shows more of her skin than I want any man to see. Because it doesn't cover any of the important parts of her. It's just a sea of red straps twisting across her body. Her beautiful tits are on full display—the perfect size for her frame, curvy but not fake.

Her nipples are pointed in the chill air, and I pretend they are that way just for me. I'd love to lick and taste them and listen to the purrs and moans leave her lips as I tease them. My eyes travel down her firm stomach, complete with the light outline of her strong abs. And her bare pussy is highlighted with two red straps on either side hiding nothing. If she's going to be sold, she's going to do it on her terms.

I feel my body responding to her, giving her all the control. My cock pushes against the zipper of my slacks.

My cock is a fucking asshole.

I'm turned on by a woman about to be sold. A woman defying us all by giving away the goods before she is even sold. I wouldn't doubt that she would drag a random man on stage and fuck him just to prove that she is in control —not us.

It's true. She wins this round. *But what about the next?*

What about when she isn't on stage?

What about when she's one-on-one with a man stronger than her?

A man who has a gun?

And a team of men working for him?

Will she always win?

Men start throwing their numbers up, pushing the bidding higher and higher, faster than they did for any of the other women as she continues to curse and spit into the audience.

Her outrage only drives the energy and bidding higher. The men all think they will be the one to break her. To control her.

And I'm just as sick as they are because I want to control her too. I want to mark that beautiful skin of hers. I want to claim that mouth and stop her from cursing anything except my name. I want to spread her legs wide and lick every drop of sweetness spreading between them.

I want her.

I want her to be mine.

I want to fight for control.

Suddenly, my hand goes up, indicating I want to bid.

"Five million, to number fifteen," Oscar says, grinning at me like we just agreed to do business together.

What am I doing?

I'm disgusting.

No, I'm saving her.

This is the only way. I have to buy her. Take her as my slave. Then I can find a way to set her free.

"Five point five million, to number twelve," Oscar says.

I grind my teeth together and then drink the rest of my scotch. The bidding has only started, and already it's higher than any of the other women's final total.

Siren is worth it. It's clear she is stronger than the other women. Her spirit is unbroken. Her desire is insatiable. Her body is flawless. She deserves to be worshipped by a king, not sold to a monster.

Her eyes track from the man who just bid on her back to me. And I swear she can see me. Not just see me, but see through me. She knows even though I claim to be bidding to save her, I'm just like every other man in this room. I'm disgusting. I'm sick. I'm a fucking bastard who doesn't deserve her.

If I win her, she will be my ultimate test. I always knew I was going to hell. I knew I was a sinner. But she would be my ultimate sin. She would confirm the darkness in my heart. Because I'm not sure I could resist her. And she knows it.

It doesn't stop my hand from raising again.

"Six million, to number fifteen."

I stare at my opponent across the room, but I can't make out his face in the darkness. I don't know how high he's willing to go. I don't know how much money he has or is willing to spend on Siren.

But I'm determined to win. She's mine, not his. I'm willing to bid everything I have on her; I just hope it's enough to win her.

7

———

SIREN

"Seven million. Really? You bastards think that's all I'm worth?" I shout out at their disgusting faces.

I hear chuckles and whistles as I reveal more of my body to them. But I don't care. I want whoever buys me to know he doesn't own my body. I've already shown myself to every man in the room. If I could have every man touch me, fuck me, ruin me for my new owner, I would. But Oscar would never allow that to happen, so I don't try.

I just strut around the stage, acting like I own it, cursing, and flipping them off every chance I get. Which only makes the crowd cheer more.

What am I doing? Why am I making more money for these assholes?

Because it hides my fear, it makes me feel powerful—in control. And it's the only thing I have left right now that's mine.

My dignity is gone.

Soon my strength, my choices, and my body will be too.

This moment is the last of any control. So I'm going to make it my most powerful.

There are only two men left bidding on me.

My fate will soon be decided.

And I don't know which man to cheer for. I don't even know who the two men are. The darkness covers their faces from me. The candlelight on the table is barely enough to make out the light of the men's eyes.

But even if I could see their faces, they are both monsters. One might be less evil than the other, but that is the best I can hope for. Otherwise, they wouldn't be here.

"Eight million."

Holy fuck.

My mouth drops open. The last woman went for five million. They are bidding eight on me and don't show any signs of slowing down.

What will be expected of me for eight million dollars?

What sexual acts will be required of me?

Will I have to fuck other men? Or will I be the buyer's prized possession?

Will he keep me alive longer because he paid more, or will he enjoy ruining me faster because he thinks I can't be broken?

The room stills as the two men continue to go back and forth, bidding against each other in half a million increments. Eight point five million. Nine million. Nine point five. Ten.

At the rate they are going, it doesn't seem like either of them will stop.

I don't move onstage. I don't flip them off or curse. I'm frozen. It's only now do I wish I was still wearing my robe to cover up.

None of the men's focus is on me; it's on the two remaining bidders. It's a game. And I can hear the bets from the other men in the room about who is going to win me.

Win me—ha. I'd like to see a man try to 'win me.' It can't be done. I'm not a possession.

"Twelve million," Oscar shouts.

The room falls silent; we all turn our heads in the direction of the other man. He leans back, out of the candlelight of the table. He's alone. He didn't bring a guard or companion to help him discuss. And I haven't seen him reach for his phone to secure more funds. He's doing this completely on his own.

Finally, I see the man lead forward until the green of his eyes flickers in the candlelight.

Gorgeous.

Consuming.

Evil.

Just the kind of man I would be attracted to if we met in a club. The wrong kind of man. The dangerous kind. The kind who will destroy me the second he gets the chance.

That's what is so fucked up about this. If he had just asked me out at a bar—bought me a drink, I would have ended up in his bed for less than the twenty bucks he'd spend on drinks. He could have gotten me with a pleasant exchange of words.

I enjoy sex. I would have spread my legs and tried any weird fantasy he had. Instead, he's dropping a small fortune, ensuring his place in hell, and fucking with my life.

I should thank him, though. Because if the other scenario had happened and he was a good lay, I might have gone out with him again. I might have fallen in love with him before I realized what a monster he is. This way, there is no chance of me falling in love. No chance of a broken heart. Just a broken leg if I don't behave.

"Twenty million," the bidder says in a deep, gravelly

voice. The kind of voice that says this ends now. I'm already his, and he won't let any other man win.

Oscar drops his mic, and silence turns to murmuring. Every man in this room has money. Every man in this room could drop that kind of money to buy me if they wanted to, but these men also like a bargain. They like a good deal, and they won't spend a fortune on one woman when they could buy five for the same price.

I let my eyes drop, making sure my pussy hasn't turned to gold or something, and that's why this man is bidding so high. But it hasn't. I don't have a clue why he thinks I'm so special to him.

Everyone turns their head to the other bidder, waiting to see what he'll do.

"Twenty-five million," he says casually, but I can hear the fear in his voice. This is as high as he can go. He won't bid again.

"Thirty," the other man says almost immediately.

Heads snap back and forth, giving me whiplash.

"Thirty million going once."

Silence.

"Twice."

Nothing.

"Sold."

Sold—that word is going to change my life. Most likely for the worse. But maybe I can find a way to use the situation to my advantage. I was just sold for $30 million. *I'm valuable. Use it.*

Before I realize what's happening, two of the guards have me by my arms and are forcing me off stage.

I try to speak, but one look from the guard who has been relatively nice so far shuts me up. I guess when you are worth thirty million dollars, no one lets you talk or walk or do anything on your own—at least not until the transaction has been made.

My robe is shoved at me.

"Put it on," the guard says.

I do, happy to have clothes on again. I look around and realize I wasn't brought back to the cage where I was held with the other girls. I'm back in the dressing room, except this time there are no beauticians waiting to style me. This time it's just me and the two guards.

"What happens now?" I ask as I tie the sash tightly around my waist and fold my arms across my chest.

"We wait for the money to be deposited. Then you will go to your new owner," the guard says.

"I'm not property. You can't just sell me."

He grins. "We already did."

Fight—that is who I am. I fight.

I don't care that these men have more muscle in a single-arm than I do in my entire body. I don't care that they have guns while I only have nails for a weapon. None of that will stop me from fighting.

I run full force in the guard's direction—angry, pissed, and unconfined. At the last second, I kick my foot up, using the pointed heel of my shoe to dig into his groin.

I hit my target.

I grin as he doubles over in pain.

I hear the other guard coming at me from behind, and I elbow him, hearing the whoosh of the blood spilling from his nose when I break it. I feel invincible in this moment. I can take on two grown men, no problem. Where I come from, you learned to be scrappy or you didn't survive. I'm a survivor.

I'll sneak out the back and never return.

I'll hot-wire a car and then steal a boat. I'll be gone from this god-forsaken island. *I'll be free.*

I reach for one of the men's guns, when a deadly voice stops me.

"I wouldn't do that if I were you."

My hand falls at his words. *What the fuck?*

I don't let men control me. I don't let a voice like that penetrate my armor. But his does. His pushes through my outer shell and cracks through like lightning splitting a tree in half. He splits my soul.

I swallow and then reach again, pushing his stupid voice down.

"Stop, Siren."

My hand freezes midair.

Stop listening to him. But there is something so commanding in his tone. Something that makes me want to listen to him. His voice convinces my heart he knows what's better for me than I do. *It's a lie.* My brain knows it, but my heart is easily tricked.

I turn slowly and come face to face with the man who will haunt me the rest of my life, even though I already know from his voice who he is.

"You can leave," Zeke says to the two guards.

"Yes, sir," they both answer before leaving Zeke and me alone in the room.

For a moment, I think Zeke might be my savior. He may have bought me to set me free. But no man spends thirty million on a woman just to set her free.

Maybe he does?

Maybe this man is good?

Maybe he realized he owed me after I saved his life?

A life for a life.

"You owe me," I say, raising my hope. I shouldn't do it.

I've been burned by too many men before. I've learned better than to trust a man. I'd be better off trusting a weasel.

"I owe you nothing."

Damn, his voice vibrates through me. A wisp of his hair falls out of the man bun in front of his face. His eyes darken. His jaw tenses. And his lips hide whatever truth he dares to never speak.

I burn down his walls with the glare in my eyes. But he doesn't move. Or flinch or show any weakness.

"I saved your life."

He shakes his head. "Julian Reed saved me. You merely transported me from the middle of the ocean to this island. I owe you a voyage to a destination not of your choosing."

I frown. "What? That makes no sense."

He steps forward. His presence fills the tiny closet of a room. I want to back away, but I don't dare show weakness. His body towers over my much smaller frame. He's a giant compared to most men. He has at least a good foot on me, even in the heels. And he fills out a suit like no man I've ever seen.

But I know he's not comfortable in it. He's not a suit kind of man. I've seen the callouses on his hands. He prefers work to commanding, although he's good at leadership. *He's probably good with his hands too.*

He cocks his strong head sitting on his thick, veiny neck. *Jesus, this man is huge.*

"Doesn't it, though? You are the reason I'm on this fucking island. You're the reason I now owe a debt to Julian. You are the reason I was in the right place to buy you."

"You can't just buy me! I'm not for sale!"

He snaps his jaw shut. "I just did, sweetheart. I just fucking did."

I stand on my tiptoes, trying to look taller. "I will never

obey you. I will never be yours. I never lie. I always tell the truth. I will destroy you before you ever lay a hand on me."

He studies me a moment. "I'm sure you believe every word you are saying, but only time will tell who will end up destroying who."

Zeke turns around and starts walking for the door. "Come," he says, without looking back at me, barking orders like a dog.

If he thinks he can just order me around, he's wrong.

He walks out the door.

I stay.

But then I hear the cries of the women in the building. Zeke may be a monster, but so far, he hasn't touched me. He hasn't beaten me. He hasn't threatened me.

I'll follow him, but only because if I stay, the men who will claim me are worse.

I exit and find Zeke holding the door open to the parking lot.

"I'm not a patient man, Siren. I paid thirty million dollars for the pleasure of ordering you around. I suggest you follow my orders in a more timely fashion."

I grit my teeth together. "Or what? You'll punish me?"

"Yes, Siren. You may always tell the truth, but I always keep a promise. I owe you a debt. You took me hundreds of miles to the nearest island. Someday, I'll repay the favor. Until then, you're mine to do as I please."

"And what do you please?"

"Right now, I want you to shut your smart mouth and get into the car."

He holds open the door of his beat-up truck.

I frown. So much about this man I don't understand. He has thirty million dollars to just blow. And yet he drives around a crappy truck. His suit is obviously a rental, he fills it out, but it's not properly tailored. This man is hiding something, and I'm going to figure it out.

I climb into the passenger side of the truck, choosing to pick my battles when it comes to Zeke. The man I saved. The man who will ruin my life. I should have known he was a jackass like every other man.

8

ZEKE

WHAT AM I DOING? My mind races as I drive down the gravel road in the dark through the middle of the island. The truck jostles back and forth roughly with each spin of the wheel. I've cracked the windows to let in the cool, salty air. The air conditioning barely works on this truck, and I didn't think I'd live here long enough to bother fixing it.

I'm treating Siren like I own her. *But do I really have a choice?*

If I started treating her like the princess she is, then Julian would start to get suspicious.

But could I treat her like a human? Tell her I only bought her to save her?

I chance a glance over at her. She sitting as far back as she can get in the seat, her legs are crossed, causing the robe to hike up dangerously high on her thigh until I can almost see the red, strappy number underneath. She's still wearing the pointed heels, but I think it's because she knows she can use them as a weapon, not because they're comfortable.

I was shocked when I entered the room and found her beating up on the two guards. She has skills—training someone taught her. She knows how to use her body as a weapon. She's dangerous. I will have to be careful with her.

But the most surprising thing is her fearlessness, even now that she's sold. She's mine, and yet she's only sitting as far away from me as possible because she's disgusted, not because she's scared.

I envy her. I want to live my life completely unafraid. Another quality that makes her dangerous.

"Fasten your seatbelt," I bark at her.

She gives me a dirty look. "Why? We are going twenty miles an hour. There are no other cars on the road at this time of night. I think I'll be fine. And don't pretend to care about my safety."

"I want to protect my investment. Buckle. Your. Seatbelt," I growl, hating how she defies me. *Can't she see I'm only trying to help her? Keep her safe?*

She flips me off. *Apparently not.*

I consider my next move. I could force her. I could do it myself. Or I could convince her to see things my way.

I choose option number three. I need her to obey me because she has no other choice. I need her to stop fighting every little order if I'm ever going to figure out how to save her.

I can't tell her the truth. *At least, not yet.*

Julian could have this truck bugged. The home I rent from him is surely bugged. He's a paranoid man who doesn't trust anyone, and he thinks I'm hiding something. I am, just not what he thinks. And until I'm free of him, I can't risk telling her the truth.

I press on the gas, going faster than safe on the bumpy, unpaved road. Siren is thrown up from her seat, until she's gripping the ceiling to keep her head from bumping into it.

"What are you doing?" her voice breathy.

Damn, I like the sound of her voice.

"Driving."

"No, you're trying to get us killed."

I shake my head as I put one hand out the window, feeling the wind as I pick up more speed. "I like to feel the wind."

"Slow down."

"I don't follow your orders. I give the orders. And you will find I only give orders once." I drive faster, watching Siren be thrown around in the truck. She's barely hanging on now. Her hands are gripping the seat, the ceiling, the frame of the window—anything she can hold onto to keep her in the car instead of bouncing out of it.

"You've made your point. Slow down," she hollers, still not giving in to my orders.

I drive faster, purposefully losing control more as I drive, running over several bushes and getting dangerously close to several trees as we bounce down the hill.

"Fuck," Siren curses when I turn head-on toward a large palm tree.

She reaches for her seatbelt almost automatically. I don't think she even realizes that she is giving into my command. As soon as she has the belt buckled, I swerve away.

"Are we dead? Did you hit it?" She asks, her eyes closed tightly, and her red lips turned ghost white.

I smile, liking her afraid, relying on me.

"Nope, we are still very much alive."

"Dammit."

She slowly opens her eyes.

"Are you going to slow down, now?"

I step on the gas. She doesn't get a reward for doing what I asked her to do five minutes after I asked it.

She sighs and grips the seatbelt now firmly across her chest.

Siren is feisty. She's not like any other woman I've met. She was the only woman out of a dozen to completely own the stage, to not let us take control of her.

She's the only woman I've ever met who doesn't want me for my money, protection, or access to my hotter, richer best friends.

Because you bought her, you idiot. That's the only reason she's in this car. A woman like her wouldn't look twice at a man like me. I have money sure, but not enough to please her. I don't have any power. I work for a powerful man. I protect. I risk my life for others. I could never fully be hers.

"What's your last name, Siren?" I ask.

She gives me the finger, her signature move.

"Where are you from? Do you live on the island?"

She raises her eyebrows at me. "You really think I'm going to answer your questions?"

"Yes."

"Why?"

"Because if you don't, there will be consequences."

She rolls her eyes. "I'm not afraid of your consequences. We aren't always going to be in a car where you can just pick up speed to get me to do what you want."

"No, but I can think of other ways to get you to do what I want." My eyes threaten her with danger, but I would never physically hurt her. I've never hit a woman, and I don't plan on doing it now. But Siren doesn't know that. And right now, I need her terrified. I need her to stop resisting and let me save her.

She goes quiet.

Good, maybe my threat worked.

"Are you married?" I ask, hoping to god she isn't.

Wait...what? Why do I care if she's married? If she is, it would be easier for me, not harder. I could just drop her off with her husband. She would become his problem to take care of, no longer my concern.

"You've never done this before, have you?" Her eyes focus on me.

I swallow hard but don't answer.

She smiles. "What is *your* full name, Zeke?"

I clench my jaw.

"Where are you from?" she asks.

"Are you married?" she asks.

She leans back, smiling smugly, thinking she's won.

She has.

But she won't again.

I turn the wheel hard, driving hard into a small ditch on the side of the road.

She squeals crazily with the fear of death in her eyes.

Then suddenly, we stop as I slam on the breaks.

"You're insane," she pants, holding her hand over her heart as she tries to catch her breath.

I grab her wrist, needing her to look at me, needing her to take me seriously.

Of course, there's a fucking spark at our touch.

We both stare down at the surge going back and forth between our skin. *How is it that the first woman I've felt butterflies for is also a woman I can't have?* I fucking bought her, even if I save her, even if I get her to freedom eventually, she won't forgive me for this. She'll always view me as an asshole.

And I will have to treat her like one until I can find a way to set her free. I don't have a choice. Julian will be watching my every move. And he'll kill us both if he thinks we aren't on his side.

But it doesn't stop my heart from doing fucking somersaults in my chest at her touch. *Maybe when I set her free, I could seduce her? I could court her? Make her fall for me by bringing her flowers, chocolates, do all the romantic things I used to be good at? Maybe that would be enough for us to have a chance?*

I lean in close, until I'm all but kissing her. She licks her lips in anticipation of a kiss that will never come. I'm in control here, not her. She doesn't get to decide my actions. I give a command; she follows it. Or there will be consequences.

"What is your last name?" I ask, my voice booming so loudly it even scares even me.

"Martinez."

"Where are you from?"

"Costa Rica."

"Are you married?"

She holds up her left hand. There is no ring or tan line where one used to sit. She's not married.

I release my grip, and we both take a deep breath, like it's a race to get all the oxygen we can before the other takes all of it.

I stare at her. Consuming all of the information she gave me. *Siren Martinez. From Costa Rica, not here. She's not married.*

That last fact warms my cold heart more than it should. She's not married, *but that doesn't really make her yours.* I don't have a real claim on her. What I have is temporary. All we have is chemistry. And fucked up debts to each other. And half-truths and lies.

We could never have a real relationship even after all of this is over.

Even though she isn't married, I'm sure she has a life waiting for her in Costa Rica.

And I have a life waiting for me in Miami.

We would never work.

I grip the steering wheel again; my point made—if she doesn't follow my command, there will be consequences. This one was simple. I scared the shit out of her with just my voice. I may not hit her, but I can find other consequences for her not bending to my will.

She doesn't know that I won't physically hurt her, but she's a smart woman. She will quickly figure it out if I'm not careful, and then she will try to run. And if she runs, Julian could find her before I do. And he's a real monster. The kind that will hit a woman. The kind who will rape her. Torture her. Kill her.

My eyes water thinking about any man hurting her. I don't know how I've already grown attached to her. *Was it because she saved me? Did I fall in love with the sound of her voice when she sang to me? Her skin when she touched me? Did I grow soft watching her on stage? Or was it this moment watching her do everything to defy me that made me fall for her?*

I don't know. But my heart definitely has a soft spot for her. That's my problem. I let people in too easily. And then I get fucking hurt. But Siren is innocent. She has a big heart. She wouldn't have saved me in the ocean if she was a cold criminal. I owe her my life.

When I get to my house, I'll get to work on debugging it, so I can eventually tell Siren the truth and form a plan to get her off this island—to get us both off this island. But until then, I will have to make Siren fear me. Fear will keep her weak, malleable. Fear will break her spirit. Every time she fears me, it will hurt. But it's the only way to protect her.

9
———

SIREN

ZEKE TURNS the car down a familiar road. The last road on the island I want to be on. A road I've traversed before. A road that became my most painful mistake. A road that led me to be sold as a sex slave.

I shift uncomfortably in my seat as the seat belt constricts across my body. I can't breathe. I can't go back. *Not here...*

I squeeze my eyes shut, hoping to block out the impending panic attack. But it's too late to stop it. The panic lives in me now.

"Siren?"

Zeke's voice breaks through the fog. It's so calming and assuring. His voice can stop the panic; his alone has that kind of power.

My eyes open cautiously, looking into his profound, intimidating eyes.

He narrows his gaze, trying to figure out what I'm hiding behind my panicked eyes. But I'll never tell. I'll keep my secrets.

But I hope Zeke spills his.

His truth is the key to escaping. *Who is Zeke? What makes him tick? Where did he come from? What motivates him? Is his heart as evil as every other man's on this island?*

I need the answers. Because with the answers comes power. I can take back control. I can earn back my freedom.

Zeke turns his attention back to the road as my breathing calms at his command. But he didn't order me to breathe. He didn't instruct me to be calm. My body responded to his on its own.

Fuck me—why does my body have to be attracted to such a cruel man? Now that his gaze is off of me, I almost want it back. I forget about any panic and only feel him. His stare makes my toes curl, my heart flutter, and my lips wet.

I'm a sex slave that wants to be fucked by her master. *How sick is that?*

I won't let it happen, though. I won't let him rape me. I will fight every second. If he asked, I might give in. I like sex as much as any other warm-blooded woman. But Zeke won't ask for sex; he's the kind of man who will demand it—the kind of man I hate.

I hear the gravel change to pavement as the road changes under the tires of Zeke's truck.

I swallow the lump in my throat and turn my gaze to the most beautiful property on the island. All white—like an angel descended to make everything pure. But there is nothing pure about this place.

I want to ask if Zeke lives here, but I don't want to give away my own truths. I don't want him to know I've been here before, so I stay silent. It seems is Zeke prefers it—silence. He doesn't speak unless he has something important to say.

We drive past the main house, Julian Reed's home.

I hold my breath the entire time, hoping we aren't going

to make a stop here, praying Zeke didn't buy me just to give me to Julian. I know it's not going to happen. Julian was the one who sold me to Oscar, who, in turn, sold me to Zeke. There would be no reason for Julian to buy me back. But it still worries me until we drive past the main building.

There are dozens of buildings on the property. Most belong to Julian's servants. I don't take Zeke as a servant, but he could have become one of Julian's employees.

Lights guide our way down the paved streets until we stop at a house on the edge of the property. This one isn't lit up like the rest. It seems to be hiding in the shadows, instead of shining brightly in glory like the rest of the buildings do on the property, proudly displaying their wealth. This house is still massive, but it's hidden beneath overgrown vines. Paint is chipping on its exterior. And based on how dark it is, I wouldn't have guessed anyone lives here.

Zeke shuts off the car and steps out without a word to me.

I sit in the car as he walks around the front of the truck, still not looking at me. I expect him to open my door and escort me inside, but he doesn't. He just walks tall and confidently toward the front door of the house. His ass is swaying nicely in his suit pants. He opens it, not needing a key. Apparently, he doesn't lock the door. He walks inside, still not giving me any attention.

Maybe he forgot about me?

Maybe he wants me to run so he can chase me? Punish me?

I don't know what game Zeke is playing at.

He hasn't given me an order.

And yet, every bone in my body is begging me to get out of the car and follow him inside.

I could run, try to escape. But I wouldn't dare, not with

Julian Reed lurking nearby. Zeke can't be worse than him. *Right?*

I saved Zeke's life, even if Zeke doesn't see it that way—I did. That has to count for some kindness on his part.

I fold my arms. *Maybe I'll just stay right here in this truck?* Zeke can't hurt me if I don't follow him inside.

Car lights from the road flash in my direction. And suddenly, I don't want to be alone anymore. I want inside.

I jump out of the car and half walk, half run inside the open door. Convincing myself that for the amount of money that Zeke paid, he will protect me. At least until he gets what he wants from me.

I pant heavily as I look around the foyer of Zeke's house for him. But I don't find him immediately.

I hear car tires squeal behind me. I sense an approaching man. I feel the danger nearing.

I need Zeke.

My eyes widen as I try to search, but I can't see in the dark. And I have no idea where the light switches are or if they will even work. *Maybe this isn't even his house? Maybe this is just the dungeon he plans on keeping me in?*

I grip the edges of my robe between my breasts, holding it tighter to my body.

"Zeke?" I ask into the shadows.

A light flickers on as Zeke appears in front of me. He's leaning against a pillar, his arms folded across his chest. He's lost his suit jacket already, his tie is gone, and his collar has been loosened, exposing the dark hair of his chest. His sleeves are rolled up until I see the start of his familiar tattoos. I remember them covering his body from when I saved him.

"Yes, Siren. Did you need something?" he asks smugly. *He's won.* He's showing me he has the power—the control. I followed him inside, and he didn't even have to say a single word.

I look like a desperate woman who wants to be controlled. I look weak—vulnerable. *And I fucking hate it.*

There is a knock at the door, and Zeke looks from me to the door. Like I might run to the man behind the door for help. He doesn't know the only man in the world who can truly terrify me is behind that door. I would trust Zeke time and time again over Julian.

Zeke doesn't give me an order, but he senses my fear. And he feels me move behind him, using him like a human shield as he goes to the door. I consider running and hiding, but I don't have the chance before Zeke opens the door.

I take a deep breath and then puff out my chest, determined to not let Julian see my fear.

"Julian, what do you need? I wasn't expecting you at such a late hour. I thought you had a client you needed to attend to," Zeke says, not showing Julian any respect.

Interesting—everyone shows Julian respect. In fact, I've never heard anyone call Julian anything other than Mr. Reed.

"I saw your truck drive in just as I got back, and I wanted to have a chat about how your meeting with Oscar went," Julian answers as he steps inside, pushing Zeke back even though Zeke never invited him in.

Zeke doesn't relent. And the two men's shoulders collide in a show of testosterone and power.

Zeke gives Julian an angry look as Julian smirks.

I'm not sure which man won, but clearly, neither of them plans on backing down.

Zeke doesn't bother to shut the door. I hope that means he isn't planning on letting Julian stay long.

Julian spots me, and my world stops.

The evil glint in his eyes brings me back to that night. The night I met him and became acquainted with the man, the monster, the devil. That was the night I learned just how vile he truly is.

Julian runs his tongue over his bottom lip as if remembering that night as well.

"And who is this beauty? Oscar said you had bought yourself a little treat at the event; I just didn't expect you to buy this exotic creature," Julian says.

Zeke studies Julian carefully and then my reaction to his words.

My fist tightens around the robe until my knuckles are white. Anger heats my cheeks and straightens my back until I'm at eye level with Julian in my heels. But fear—fear licks at my heart.

Julian notices the anger.

But Zeke, he notices the fear.

"Yes, I couldn't resist her," Zeke says. The way he says it seems like I'm the one with the power, but he's just teasing. It's clear he doesn't plan on letting me have any.

Julian's attention flickers back to Zeke as Zeke walks in front of me.

I exhale a small breath when Julian can no longer get a direct view of my body. I don't know why Zeke is standing in front of me. *Did he see the way Julian was looking at me? Is Zeke possessive? Does he not want to share me? Or is he protecting me?*

"Oscar seems to think I'm the man for the job. I'll have the deal closed and the shipment handled by the end of the month," Zeke says.

"Yes, Oscar told me. It seems that by buying the slut, you ensured your loyalty to him. Especially since you were the highest bidder of the night," Julian says.

"As I've said before, I'm the best. I do good work. You have nothing to worry about. These house calls aren't necessary," Zeke says.

Julian steps closer to Zeke, but I realize it's so he can look at me, not him. "I didn't stop by because I didn't believe you could do your job. I consider you a friend, Zeke. I thought we could discuss how our nights went over a drink and enjoy your new pet."

That word—*pet*. It's like being pummeled with bullets when he says that word. I hate it. I never thought I could hate a word, but I hate that word.

Zeke laughs, completely unaffected and unaware of how Julian is gazing at me like I'm his, not Zeke's. I see the promise in Julian's eyes; he will come for me. He will remind me of our night together. He isn't finished with me.

"Goodnight, Julian."

Julian looks from me to Zeke. He's been dismissed— without an explanation of why he can't stay.

My mouth gapes. It's clear Zeke is currently working for Julian, but he doesn't let Julian boss him around. He's his own man, with his own desires and own control on life.

Julian frowns, but he doesn't argue with Zeke. He'll save his fight for another night. At least, that's what his eyes promise me.

Fuck.

Zeke doesn't walk Julian to the door. He stands solid, an unmoving statue. He won't let any man come into his house and order him around, that much is clear.

"The door," Zeke says, his voice booming as Julian exits.

For a moment, I don't think Julian is going to shut the door. I think he's going to leave it open. But at the last second, he changes his mind and closes the door behind him.

Huh? Maybe I'm not the only one under Zeke's spell.

Zeke turns and looks at me. He looks menacing, like a beast. He's muscle, tattoos, and hair. The suit he wears is practically bulging off of his body. It's clear he doesn't belong in it. He's too manly for a suit. Too big. Too much beast.

"Come," he says as he starts walking.

I consider defying him. But Julian is too close. I won't defy him when the alternative is Julian.

Zeke walks down the hallway, but he doesn't turn on any lights. He just walks. And I follow, desperate to feel more in control.

I want out of these clothes. I want to wear something more respectable. I want out of this caked-on makeup. I want a bubble bath. I want food in my belly. And a bed to sleep in.

But I doubt I will get any of that. I'm sure he's leading me to some shackles for my wrists and ankles. Then to my cage. And if he isn't a patient man...he'll try to rape me.

I start looking for a weapon. Something I can use to prevent that from happening. But it's so freaking dark I can't see anything. I assume that's part of his plan to keep me captive.

Suddenly, he stops.

"Sit," he commands.

I look around but can't see a foot in front of my face. I doubt he wants me to sit in a chair anyway. So I start to sit on the floor.

"Stop."

I stop mid crouch.

I hear the scraping of a chair being pulled out. "Sit here."

I feel for the chair he's placed in front of me and take a seat, I realize at a table.

My heart thumps, trying to guess what is going to happen next, but I can't figure Zeke out. He's the most mysterious man I've ever met. When I saved him, I thought he could be different. I thought he could be one of the good ones, but it turns out he's working for Julian, and I'm now his slave. I can't gleam any more since he hardly speaks, though.

I hear him banging around, opening drawers and cabinets. *What is he searching for? Rope? A knife? Something to hurt me with?*

I hold my breath as I feel around on the table, but I don't find anything for a weapon.

Finally, Zeke returns, plopping something on the table in front of me.

"Eat."

"What?"

He sighs, taking the seat next to me. "Is your hearing bad? Or do you just like asking questions you already know the answer to?"

I frown, even though I doubt he can see it. "I don't like being ordered around."

"And I don't like having to work out, but it doesn't stop me from doing it every day. Now eat."

I cross my arms. "You working out and me taking orders from you aren't exactly comparable."

"Eat," he huffs, like he doesn't have the energy for this.

I grin. I'm learning something about him already. Talking must wear him down. If I can exhaust him, he'll be too tired to rape me. He might even let his guard down and tell me more about himself.

"How do I know you haven't poisoned it?"

"Why would I spend millions of dollars on you only to poison you?"

"Fine. How do I know you won't drug me?"

"You don't. But you're hungry, so you don't really have a choice."

"How do you know I'm hungry?" My stomach growls, giving me away.

"Because you are. Oscar wanted you to look your best so he could earn top dollar. That means skinny, not bloated with food. You're hungry. Eat."

"I can't eat in the dark."

He growls loudly.

It shakes every nerve in my body, causing me to tremble. But not in fear—in excitement. I like the way his voice sounds. I like his commanding echo. If we were in a consensual relationship, I would want him to boss me around in the bedroom. But we aren't, which means I have to fight.

"Then, I guess you won't eat."

I hear the sound of him chewing his food.

And I stare into the darkness at the table in front of me. *Why does he like living in the darkness?* Just another question without an answer.

I want to defy him. I want to go without eating, but I'll need my strength to face him. To have a chance against him.

So carefully, I feel around on the table until I find a fork. Then I move it around on my plate, and I stab a piece of food and lift it to my mouth. I smell it hesitantly—broccoli.

I curl my lips down in disappointment. I could go for some French fries or a burger or pizza—something heavy on the carbs. But of course, mister zero percent body fat and all muscle only eats vegetables.

But once I put the broccoli in my mouth, I don't care. It practically melts in my mouth. I don't know how it's cooked so well. I put my fork down on the plate again, but realize I'm stabbing meat instead of broccoli this time.

I frown. I'm going to have to nibble on the meat with my teeth. I'm sure he didn't give me a knife.

Hesitantly, I feel around on the other side of my plate, and there I find the sharp edge of a steak knife.

I have a weapon!

As quickly as I lift it, I feel Zeke's hand grip my wrist.

I freeze. At his touch, my hair rises on my arms, wanting to feel more of him. My breath catches, and my heart slows. I bite my lip, waiting to hear what he says.

"You show your thoughts easily, Miss Martinez. If you are planning on killing me with this knife, I suggest you have a plan to kill Julian as well. Because the only thing standing between him and you is me." He releases my wrist and goes back to eating. I decide it's best to only use the knife to cut my steak instead of Zeke's throat—at least for the time being.

How did Zeke so clearly read my thoughts? No one can ever read me. I'll have to be more careful, so he doesn't learn my secrets before I learn his.

We continue to eat in silence. Zeke finishes eating long before I do, and I can feel his heavy gaze on me as I keep eating, even though we are eating in the dark. I'm glad it's dark, so I can't see the look in his eyes. *What would I find there if I could see his eyes? Want? Lust? Desire?* I don't want my body to react to any of those feelings. I'm not in a place to handle them. So I just focus on eating.

A moment after I finish, Zeke grabs my plate and silverware and whisks them away. Again he doesn't speak, but I hear his heavy footsteps. He's walking away, and before I can make a cognitive decision, I'm following him.

Zeke didn't give me an order, but I'm already eager to

follow his unspoken commands. *What will happen when he actually gives me an order? What then? How much of my soul will I lose while Zeke holds me hostage?* Not much, since I barely have any soul left to lose. I'm barely hanging on to who I am as it is.

I'm usually defiant. I'm a fighter. I will fight if Zeke tries to harm me, but somehow I've turned into an obedient dog, trying to figure out how to please my new master without him even speaking a word. It's because I'm exhausted and just want to sleep in peace. I don't want to get hurt. I don't want to face Julian.

Zeke walks through a hallway, again in the dark. I hear him open a door at the end of the hallway and step inside. I follow, assuming it's the cage he plans on keeping me in.

But when I walk inside and see the moonlight shining through a large window, I'm shocked to see the most beautiful cage he could have created for me.

A large king-sized bed is the focus of the room, with shiny white sheets sparkling in the moonlight. The floor is dark wood, in deep contrast with the bed, making it look like it's floating on water. The windows are large and look out over the cliffside to the ocean beyond—the only place where I feel at home.

I look to Zeke, who is opening a dresser drawer.

"Is this my room?" I ask, my throat dry as I speak. It doesn't make sense if it is. *Is he buttering me up with a soft, beautiful bed before he rapes me? Or does he prefer to do his damage in the clean white sheets?*

"No."

No? Then what am I doing here if it isn't my room?

I start slowing backing away, not liking being in the same room with Zeke when there is a bed he could easily destroy me on.

He closes the drawer and faces me just as I get to the door. He doesn't seem surprised that I'm trying to escape. He doesn't draw a gun or try to prevent me from running in any way. He seems in complete control standing there facing me.

"Leaving?" he asks with an amused expression.

"Yes. If this isn't my room, then I shouldn't be in here." I take another step back toward the door, but face Zeke as I do it. I won't ever turn my back on my enemy.

"Who says I'm giving you any of my rooms?" Zeke answers.

I narrow my eyes. "Then where will you keep me?" *Please tell me there isn't a dungeon or cage somewhere on this property.* I'm starting to think Zeke didn't go to that auction planning on buying me, but something changed, and he did. He's not prepared for me.

Zeke's eyes cut to the bed.

I swallow. He wants me in his bed. He's not going to wait to rape me. He's going to take what he wants right here, right now.

He tosses something at me, and I catch it automatically.

"Put it on," he says before he turns around.

I glance at my hands and realize it's a T-shirt—one of Zeke's T-shirts. I'd rather sleep in this than what I'm wearing, but I doubt I'll be sleeping at all tonight.

When I look up, I see Zeke undressing. He's slowly unbuttoning his shirt and pulling it out from his pants. But he isn't facing me. He's giving me the privacy to change without him looking. So I take advantage. I disrobe and remove my uncomfortable, strappy number and then slip the T-shirt over my head. I feel more comfortable in the shirt that hangs down to just above my knees, but I do wish I had underwear to sleep in.

Zeke is still undressing away from me. His shirt is gone now, and he's working on his pants.

My teeth scrape over my bottom lip as I take his backside in—strong and masculine. His hair is still up in a man bun on top of his head, and it gives me an unobstructed view of every muscle and tattoo on his back.

Most of the bidding men in that auction room were disgusting, gross, unfit monsters. But Zeke has the body of a god; he didn't need to buy one in order to have his choice of women. Tattoos are inked into his back, and when he drops his pants, I groan at the sight of his tight ass in his Calvin Kleins, fitting to his muscular ass like a second layer of skin.

Turn around. Show me your package.

He does, and my eyes bulge. *Holy hell!* I've never seen a package so perfectly formed beneath a man's boxer briefs. But his has me mesmerized. I want to unwrap him and see what's underneath. I want to turn him on and see how big his erection can grow. I want—

"My eyes are up here, Siren."

Fuck, I've been caught.

I glare at him. "Just getting a good look so I know where to aim when I cut off your dick. Because I will knife you before I ever let you stick your cock anywhere near me."

He cocks his head. "Really? Because the heat in your eyes, the flush in your cheeks, and drool pooling in the corner of your mouth tells me you'd rather ride my cock than cut it off."

I grit my teeth as steam boils inside me. *How can he be so infuriatingly good at reading me?* I always hide my emotions. It's my signature trait. But not with him. With him, he sees the real me, and that terrifies me. He could discover my secret, and that would be worse than him raping me.

Zeke walks over to me, and I freeze. I try to hold my

expression so he can't tell if I'm terrified, turned on, or am about to attack him. He stops just in front of me and both of our breaths heat. He exhales into my hair, while I inhale his bare chest.

My breath rises harder in my chest, and I lick my lips in anticipation of a kiss before I remember that he owns me. He isn't going to kiss me; he's going to fuck me—destroy me, ruin me.

I glance up, and his dark eyes read mine. For a second, I think he's trying to tell me something with just his eyes, but I'm probably reading too much into it.

He reaches around me and closes the door behind me before locking it.

"You can sleep on the left side of the bed," he says before he turns and walks to the right side of the bed.

What?

I watch Zeke climb into the right side of the bed, and I swear he's snoring as soon as his head hits the pillow.

He's not going to rape me, at least not tonight.

But can I really sleep in the bed next to him?

I tiptoe over to the bed, hoping like hell I don't wake him. If I do, he might change his mind and realize he's hornier than he is exhausted.

But he doesn't stir. I glance at the floor. I could sleep there instead of in his bed. But I wouldn't get a minute of sleep; the floor is too hard. I glance at the door Zeke locked. He locked it from the inside. I could leave no problem.

But where would I go? What security measures does Zeke have in place? And how far would I get before Julian would find me? Could I sleep in a different room?

No.

I need to earn Zeke's trust. Make him fall for me. Learn his secrets. That's the best way to get free.

Stop being a fucking pussy.

I pull the slick covers back and climb into the heavenly bed. I close my eyes as my head hits the pillow, expecting to feel more petrified than I have in months. But instead, I feel the heavy pull of sleep as my heart calms next to Zeke's light snoring. He could hurt me as bad as any man ever has. He could kill me, end me. But somehow, I feel more protected than ever.

10

ZEKE

I DON'T SLEEP. How could I, with the most gorgeous, intelligent, quick-witted woman in my bed?

I pretend to snore initially, so Siren would trust me enough to sleep next to me. But it was all an act. I'm learning I can be a good actor when I want to be.

I should have locked Siren up in one of the other bedrooms. I should have tied her up with ropes. I should have ensured there is no way she could escape while simultaneously fueling my new fantasies about having Siren tied up.

But I'm not that breed of monster. The only promise I've silently made to her is not to hurt her. So I won't. I might manipulate her. I might do cruel things, but I'm only doing them to protect her. If I can avoid physically hurting her, I will.

And given her reaction to Julian Reed, there is no way she will voluntarily leave my property. She's too afraid he will hurt her. So in her mind, the safest place she can be right now is my bed, even if that confuses her. Hell, it confuses me.

It's been ages since I've been this attracted to a woman. Siren is hot, sure, but she's so much more. I want to know everything about her. I could listen to her smart mouth put me in my place all damn day. I want to know every snarky comment in her beautiful brain. And I want...hell, I'm desperate to kiss her red-stained lips. Just once, I want to fight back with my lips pressed against hers instead of riling her up with my own careful words.

There is so much I want to say to her. But I can't, not until I know Julian isn't listening to our every conversation.

And what was with Siren's reaction to Julian anyway? Yes, he's a very intimidating man. Anyone could look at him and tell that he's evil. But Siren didn't show a moment of fear on that stage when she was in a room of dozens of wealthy, horrid men. A man like Julian shouldn't scare her, unless they have history together.

It was clear they have met before. And that meeting wasn't a pleasant one. Siren doesn't even fear me—the man who bought her for millions and she thinks is going to rape her. And yet she fears Julian.

I have to find a way to get answers. But I don't want Julian to know that I realize he knows Siren. Or at least, Siren knows him. He's such a bastard he probably hurt her and then forgot about her. And when he saw her with me, he wanted to destroy her all over again.

I need answers from Siren, which is going to be hard. I also need to stay as far away from her as possible.

I glance over at the angel of a woman, perplexed that she doesn't call herself that. Sure, she has a potty mouth. And I believe her when she says she'd cut off my dick before she lets me touch her, but she's still my angel and probably my downfall into darkness.

I'm generally a good man, at least when it comes to

women. I don't lead them on. I don't date. I give them a good night or two, and then I move on. But with Siren, I know one night wouldn't be enough. I want to do dirty, offensive things to her. I want to own her, just like I paid for. I want to break her and then put her pieces back together, so she owes me a thousand unrelenting debts.

My hand reaches out, wanting to brush her strands from her face, but I stop at the last second. I can't even let myself have a taste. I have the ultimate level of self-control, but with Siren, I'm going to fall into the depths of hell after one drop. I want her too much. If I get one taste, I'll be hooked. I won't be able to keep my promises not to hurt her. And I'll become like the men I'm trying to protect her from.

So I keep my hands to myself. The less I touch her, the better.

But the longer I stay in bed with her, the less control I have on my body. Especially when she starts making adorable snoring noises in her sleep.

I have to get out of here.

I jump out of bed, not caring if I wake her. I have work to do. I have a house to debug, a debt to Julian to repay, and figuring out how to sell women while saving them at the same time. Not to mention what the hell I'm going to do with Siren to keep her safe once I've repaid my debt to Julian and ensured he won't follow me when I leave.

I grab my jeans and T-shirt from the closet and then walk down the hallway to the bathroom. Why the hell this house doesn't have a bathroom that connects to the bedroom is beyond me. Siren doesn't stir as I leave, and even if she does, she won't leave the safety of the house. I don't have to worry about her escaping.

I walk into the bathroom, flick the shower water to cold, remove my boxer briefs, and stand under the cold spray. I'm desperate for it to knock some sense into me and ease the pain of my night-long erection.

But when I look down, my cock is still hard, aching to be inside Siren.

Fucking hell.

I fall forward and put my hands on the wall of the shower. I let the cold water fall over my head and down my back and chest. I close my eyes as I pant heavily, trying to get the images of Siren out of my head.

I try to think of anything else—Julian, the old lady who gets me coffee at the cafe down the street, a peanut butter sandwich, the work I need to do to the beat-up truck. *Fucking anything*—but my cock is still hard.

I want to jack off, but I know if I do, Siren's body will be what I get off to. Her body on stage with a few tiny straps hiding only part of her skin, but not the most intimate parts.

I'm sick.

I won't pleasure myself to her being forced onto a stage for others' enjoyment.

I start thinking about all the men who saw Siren basically naked. All the men who have probably rubbed their dicks to the image of her they have branded into their heads already.

My stomach flips at that thought. I hate that any man has ever seen Siren that exposed, basically naked. And with that thought, my erection immediately disappears.

My job is to protect those I love, those I owe a debt to, those that are innocent. I owe Siren a debt. I won't let her fall into any other category.

I turn off the water, get dressed, and then walk back to my bedroom.

Siren is awake, with the covers lifted up to her chin like that will protect her from me.

"Are you hungry?" I ask.

She shakes her head.

I walk over to her side of the bed and pull a bottle of water out of the nightstand and set it next to her. I've kept a few bottles of water in the nightstand so I could take my medications the first thing in the morning.

"I'm going to work," I say.

Her eyes widen, and a smile forms behind her lips. She thinks she can plan. She can search my house to find dirt on me. But even if she did, there is nothing here. She will find no personal detail about me if she ripped this house apart room by room.

I walk to the door, though, as a plan forms to keep her safe. She's safe in my house, sure, but she's safest in this bedroom. She won't be tempted to run away if she can't see how easy it would be for her to run down the beach and away from Julian's property. Here she won't be tempted to leave.

"Enjoy your cage until I get back," I say as I close the door and pretend to lock it from the outside. But there is no lock on the outside, although she doesn't know that.

I hear her run to the door and pound on it hard.

"Zeke! Don't! Don't lock me in here!" she shouts from behind the door.

"It's for your own good. I wouldn't want you to wander and fall into the hands of a man who isn't as kind and patient as I am."

"I'm claustrophobic!"

"Good thing that room is huge then."

"What about food?"

"I asked, you said you weren't hungry. I'll be back by dinner time."

I start backing up as she keeps pounding on the door

but doesn't once test the door handle. She believes me. She truly thinks I locked her inside the room.

"Zeke...please." Her voice is soft and begging.

It should make me want to help her. I'd help any other woman who spoke to me that way. I'd tell them the truth. I'd find another way to contain them. But not with Siren. Siren's sultry plea makes my cock hard. It twists me into a one-track man who wants to devour her.

She's safer locked in my bedroom.

So I walk away and hope Siren doesn't realize the door isn't locked. She's as free as she was before she was kidnapped, but I'm not the devil she thinks I am. I'm much worse. I'm the kind who pretends to protect her but ultimately destroys her—just as soon as my beast within breaks through.

If Siren is smart, she'll run. She'll save herself before my beast escapes. Because when he does, she'll never be safe.

11

—————

SIREN

FUCKING BASTARD.

Asshole.

Buttmunch.

Jackass.

Coward.

Zeke fucking locked me in his bedroom. And it pisses me off. *I'm not an animal he can just lock up!*

But apparently, I am. That is exactly what he did. He locked me up and is holding me hostage.

And now what do I do?

He expects me to wait until he returns so he can order me around and have his way with me—I don't think so.

That sure as hell isn't happening.

My thighs clench, my nipples pebble, and my mouth runs dry just thinking about Zeke. I slept next to him all night. Somehow, my dreams were all about him. *Dreams*—not nightmares.

In them, he wasn't much different than the man I've come to know since he bought me—the strong, silent type.

He would just look at me and I could tell everything he was thinking—exactly what he wanted me to do.

And I did it. I undressed slowly. I touched myself, spread the moisture between my legs over my lips so he could see how wet I was for him. He was commanding without saying a word. And I wanted to follow his every desire.

But then I woke up. I remembered no matter how attracted I am to Zeke, I will never fuck him. For a split second, when I saved him in the water, I thought he might be the rare good guy who would never hurt a woman. But now I know the truth.

He locked me up simply because it was the easiest course of action. He knows he doesn't need to tie me up, although he might try to just for his own twisted enjoyment.

Currently, a simple lock on the door is the only thing between me and freedom.

I fold my arms over my chest as the air conditioning kicks on and chills my arms and legs. I'm still naked except for Zeke's oversized T-shirt.

I should find more clothes.

I should break down the door or one of the windows.

I should run.

But I can't.

The island is too small. Zeke could find me easily. Or Julian...I won't risk Julian finding me. So I'll stay.

I walk over to the dresser and pull out drawer after drawer until I find a pair of sweatpants. I put them on, feeling less naked, even though I have to roll the waistband several times and tie the string around my body to keep the pants up.

I may not be able to escape, but at least I can find out more about Zeke. I can gather as much ammunition possible on the man. I need him to get me off this island. I need answers.

So I dig through all of the drawers in his dresser. All I find are clean boxer briefs that somehow already smell like him. I inhale the sweet mix of ocean, fresh-cut grass, and intangible man. I find socks, T-shirts, and jeans. All I learn is that he likes his clothes casual, yet designer.

I dig through the nightstands on either side of his bed. I find water bottles, pain pills, and a tattered copy of Moby Dick. He reads apparently. Or at least he likes this particular book.

I find nothing else I might expect from a monster like him. Nothing kinky. No BDSM stuff. No handcuffs, ties, whips. I don't even find a condom. *Maybe he isn't into safe sex? Maybe he's one of those sick bastards who likes to impregnate women and then beat them until the baby no longer exists?*

Fuck.

I slam the last drawer shut, trying not to think that way anymore. *Zeke isn't an angel, but he can't be that big of a monster, can he?*

I sit back on my heels and look around the room. There is no door other than the one leading to the hallway. No closet to search through. No bathroom to rummage through. I've officially run out of things to search in the first fifteen minutes he's gone. And I've learned practically nothing about Zeke.

Wait...there is no other door! No bathroom!

I stand up and look again. That can't be right. This room is too beautiful and grand for a bathroom to not be connected to it. But there is no door. There is no place for another door to be; it would ruin the enormous ocean vista out the windows.

My belly rumbles. I place my hand on my stomach and frown. Not only do I not have any food for however many hours Zeke is gone, but I don't have a bathroom.

I sigh.

I won't let him win. He's just doing this to agitate me and rile me up, so when he returns, I'll fight harder. That's probably what his sick mind is thinking. That's why he didn't touch me last night. He knew I was too exhausted to fight hard.

I eye the big bed and climb back under the sheets. I'm not tired since I'm used to only getting a few hours at a time. And despite it not being the smartest thing I've ever done, I slept just fine with Zeke next to me all night.

My pussy pulses and my tongue runs over my lips just thinking about Zeke.

Dammit!

I can't want him. He's a horrible person. But then again, I'm always falling for the wrong men. Time and time again, I find myself lusting over a man who deserves to be thrown in prison, not in my bed.

You make bad decisions, that's why I don't let you make any decisions for us anymore, I think to my crotch.

But it's been so fucking long since a man touched me, brought me to the brink of ecstasy, pounded into me until only pleasure cascaded through me. I may not be able to find a good man, but I can find a to-be-confirmed-bad boy. A complete stranger I can fuck and abandon before I get to know him. Those are the only good guys anyway, the kind whose shit I don't know about.

For now, my fingers will have to do. I don't have anything else to do for the hours that I have to wait for Zeke to return anyway.

I lay in the middle of Zeke's bed, under the cloud-like covers. My eyes scan the room, looking for the camera I'm sure the bastard has hidden in here. The windows are hard to plant a camera on without it being noticeable. I look up at the light fixture—a strong possibility, but I don't see anything out of the ordinary to indicate a camera. Then I look to the door.

I narrow my eyes on the door handle as I try to spot anything there that shouldn't be—bingo. The screw on top of the door handle is bigger than the one below it. It appears to be more flat, more like a nail than the screw underneath. And I guarantee if I got out of bed and walked over to it, I'd be able to see a tiny lense instead of a screw.

For a moment, I consider ducking under the covers to touch myself. Keeping silent, so even if he guesses what I'm doing, he will never be able to see me. Just like he will never be able to touch me.

But what's the fun in that?

I've never been the kind of woman who shies away from owning who I am. I'm a strong, confident, sexual woman. And I own myself; no man owns me.

Pain fills my heart when I speak the words to myself, in my own head. Because I can't tell a lie, and those words are all lies.

I throw the covers off my body and push the sweatpants down off my hips before spreading my legs wide, giving the camera the perfect view of my body.

He's supposed to be working, but he might be watching me right now on his phone, and I plan on giving him one hell of a show.

I lift the shirt up off my head and then shake my locks, letting my hair fall down in my face. I bite my lip, wishing I had some red lipstick and fuck-me heels on to really bring the message home, but I don't.

I own me.

I own my body.

I own my mind.

My soul.

My heart.

No man will ever claim a single part of me as his. And even if a man does, I will fight to get every part of me back.

I arch my back and puff out my chest as my hand twists my nipple between my fingers.

I let the images come of men I've fucked before—men that were excellent in bed and hotter than gods. I don't think about what the men did to me after. How they all betrayed me. I just let their expansive chests and rippling abs fill my head. I let my mind drift over each and every one of them, like they are nothing but objects for me to get off to.

But then my mind stops and flutters to a man it shouldn't.

No!

I open my eyes, pushing him out of my brain.

I take a deep breath—and Zeke fills my nostrils. I smell him everywhere. On the pillow, the sheets. His smell turns me on.

And I know who I'll be thinking about as I pleasure myself—my fucking master.

It's wrong...so fucking wrong. But I can't stop myself from thinking about Zeke. Not when I'm dripping and I haven't even touched myself yet.

I let my hand slide down my stomach and between my thighs, I find my lips and let my long fingers rub over the whole area taking my time as moisture covers my fingers.

I look straight into the camera as one hand pleasures

myself. *This is what you are missing, bastard! This is what you'll never get! You will never touch me. Never hurt me. I have all the power here, not you.*

I rub my fingers up over my clit, as it grows more sensitive. I imagine Zeke's big hands touching the sensitive bud. His tongue lapping, as more my slave than master. But as soon as he makes me come, the roles change. I'm his.

How I would beg, plead, kiss—do anything for his cock to stretch me in that uncomfortable, delicious way his large cock is surely capable of, where most men come up short. Zeke would fill me to my limits. He's a big guy, and I've seen the outline of his partial erection. The real thing would be the stuff of dreams.

Just thinking about what Zeke could do to me if he chose to fuck me like a man instead of a monster brings me close, until I'm at the place where if I don't stop, I won't be able to stop the impending orgasm. But I don't want to stop. I want to come over and over. Until I drive him crazy. Until he knows if he fucked me tonight, I wouldn't feel anything but my own fingers on my pussy—I'd be numb to him.

As I come, I use my other hand to flip off the camera. The release as I come is huge. I feel it in every nerve in my body. It cascades down my body like a waterfall overwhelming all of my nerves in my body.

It's a big fuck you to every other man in the world. I don't need a man to make myself come. I don't need a man to make it the best orgasm of my life. I don't need a man...

Dammit, there I go lying to myself again. Because I got off to a man—Zeke.

I let the orgasm roll through me before I get up. I walk naked over to the door, and then I give the camera both of my middle fingers.

"Fuck you! I will never be yours! You will never touch

me. You will never fuck me. You don't fucking own me!" I slam my hand on the door and jump back when it creaks open the tiniest bit.

What the...?

I expect Zeke to walk through the door. *Did he choose this moment to come home?*

I swallow, realizing my little show might have been a bad idea. As much as I wanted Zeke to come home and let me out of my cage, I was safe as long as he wasn't here. With him here, I'm in danger full-time again.

I'm suddenly very self-conscious of my nakedness and fingers that smell like sex.

He won't fuck me. I won't let him.

Lies. If he wants to fuck you, what is your scrawny ass going to be able to do about it?

I stare at the door, waiting for Zeke to pull it open. He doesn't.

I push my hand on the door, and it opens.

I walk out and look at the other side of the door. There is no lock. The door only locks from the inside.

The fucking bastard—Zeke lied to me.

I hate human traffickers, and thieves, and rapists, and murderers. But liars—I hate them most of all. Other monsters show you exactly who they are. They don't hide their horns; you can tell they are the devil right from the start. But liars—they pretend to be better than all the rest. They like to play games, deceive, and trick you into a false sense of security before they rip out your heart and stab it to death.

Zeke is a human trafficker. One look at him tells me he's also a thief, a rapist, and a murderer. But I thought at least he could be honest about who he is. Instead, he'd rather play games and test me.

Fine, if he wants to play games, we will play games. But unlike him, I won't lie and cheat. I'll win while telling every damn truth I have. Even if he's too stupid to believe me —I'll win.

12

———

ZEKE

THE DAY DRAGGED, but it's finally time for me to go home. It's eight o'clock in the evening, and I know Julian has a few guests coming over to occupy the rest of his night, which means I can get the hell out of here. I'm tired of talking to Julian about contracts, men who I can trust to transport the women, and the plan for selling them. I'm tired of pretending I find Julian's way of making money admirable. Although, I never verbally agreed with him. I never said anything to the contrary—lie by omission.

Why I thought I owed Julian a debt though is ridiculous. This man is a coward and a greedy criminal. He knew I could help him, so he let his doctors treat me. He didn't save me—not like Siren did.

I should have left the island as soon as I was strong enough to go. I could be back with Enzo, Kai, and Langston by now. Or at the very least in a cabin hiding out until I healed enough to not be a burden on my friends. I shouldn't have stayed.

But I wouldn't have seen Siren again. She would have

been sold to a different man, one who would have already raped and beaten her. She'd probably already be dead.

My heart rages just thinking about what would have happened to Siren if I hadn't had been there that night, if I hadn't saved her.

I shake my head. *I haven't saved her yet.* She's not safe until she's off the island. There is something I'm missing between her and Julian. Some dark past I'm not aware of. But I'm going to find out, and Siren is going to be the one to tell me.

"Good work today, Zeke," Julian says as he takes a puff of his cigar.

I nod.

"Want to stay for a drink? I heard you drank at Oscar's, so it seems like your self-imposed sobriety has ended."

I nod. "I figured my body had done enough healing; it's time to get back to the real world. But I'll take a rain check on the drink."

Julian smiles, evilly. "Of course. You have more important things to get back to. I was surprised to see you up so early this morning at work; I assumed you had a long night breaking that one in."

My insides curl as he speaks about Siren like she's a horse needing domesticating instead of a woman. I don't give him confirmation of what I'm feeling inside.

"Need anything else before I go?" I ask instead, trying to change the subject.

Julian takes a long puff on his cigar as he rests his other hand across the back of his expensive red couch.

"No, but I plan on cashing in that rain check on Friday night."

I raise an eyebrow.

"I'm having my closest friends over then. They will be our best bets at securing buyers for the women."

I cringe on the inside. I'm going to actually do this—sell women to monsters. I don't have a choice if I want to protect my friends—if I want to protect Siren. I need to do the job, earn Julian's trust, and then get the fuck out of here.

"I'll be here then."

"Good, and bring your pet."

"Pet?" I ask automatically, not understanding what Julian is talking about, until I remember the previous night. He called Siren a pet.

"Yes, that beautiful whore you spent so much money on. Someday you'll have to tell me how you earned so much money to waste on a creature like her. But I can understand the intrigue. I understand wanting to harness that kind of power."

"I don't think she'll be up for meeting anyone so soon. Not after what I have planned for her."

Julian grins. "Just make sure she's still breathing. It doesn't matter if you've tamed her yet. Or if she's broken and bleeding. The men will be drawn to her no matter what. They will see the high-quality women we have. They will spend more money and want more of our inventory."

I try to think quickly to keep Siren at home instead of in Julian's clutches, but it's not my strong suit. I'm a methodical, careful thinker. Give me a month to make a plan, and it will run perfectly. I can protect others quickly with my body, but not my wit.

So I just nod and leave. I won't let Siren anywhere near Julian or his men. But I have a couple of days to figure out a plan.

I drive the truck home and park it in front of the house. It's time to see if Siren has escaped or not.

She's attracted to me. Her eyes speak volumes. She wants me. And she's terrified of Julian. She thinks I will protect her against him. She's right. But she doesn't get to know that.

She didn't run.

I open the front door and immediately realize I'm wrong. She fucking ran, but only after trashing my house.

Furniture is kicked over, papers are scattered everywhere, and dishes are shattered all over the floor. My eyes fume as I take in all the damage she did.

I understand she doesn't want to be a hostage, but this is unacceptable. I haven't been anything but hospitable toward her. I fed her last night. I gave her a comfy bed to sleep in. I've protected her all day from Julian. And this is how she repays me—by breaking everything in my house and then leaving.

I walk over to the liquor cabinet, hoping she didn't shatter my whiskey because I'm in desperate need of a drink. *That fucking pain in my side of a woman*—she spilled every drop and then shattered the bottle for good measure.

Other than last night, I've haven't had a drink in months. And now, when I desperately need it, she took my relief from me.

I decide to go shower and wash the anger away before I decide to search for her or not. But a creak stops me.

I look down the hallway to my right, the opposite direction of the bedrooms. And I can sense her presence without seeing or hearing her.

She's here.

She didn't run.

I take my time walking down the hallway. No one can make me rush unless I want to. And I don't fucking want to rush into that room. Because I'll break my promise not to hurt her if I do.

I take a deep breath before turning the corner to the sitting room. It's my favorite room in the house, so it doesn't surprise me Siren was drawn to it. But if she destroyed this room too, I'm going to throw her ass out, and she can figure out how to deal with Julian on her own.

The room is perfect, untouched. However, instead of being empty and mine, as usual, Siren has taken over the room as her's.

I stand in the doorway and growl, making my feelings known without having to speak.

Her eyes drift up from the book in her lap and the glass of red wine in her left hand.

"You going to speak, or are you just going to stand there?" she asks, with a knowing smirk on her lips. I'm starting to believe her now when she told me she wasn't an angel.

"I'm not the one who needs to speak. You do," I say, still standing in the doorway. If I enter the room, I'll lose my temper, and I have no idea what I'm capable of doing to her. I've never been this pissed off with a woman before. She ignites feelings I didn't even know I could have.

She raises an eyebrow and then casually takes a sip of her wine. "I don't think so. I think you have things you need to say first."

I lose it.

I'm to her in one giant step. I shove the book out of her hand and down the glass of wine, needing alcohol in my system to settle my nerves as I press her deeper into the chair.

Her eyes bulge as she grips the armrests of the chair.

"You destroyed my house! Do you know how much

damage you caused? Do you know how much money I've already spent on you? How much troub—" I stop myself before I reveal my real thoughts.

She glares at me. "You lied to me! You said you locked me in the bedroom and didn't actually lock the door. You made me feel like an idiot. You locked me in a room with no bathroom or food. You made this all into one big game. This is my life! And I won't be lied to."

I laugh in her face. Breaking down was a mistake, because it causes me to move closer to her and straddle her in the chair. And now I can smell her. And she smells like sex.

What did my little vixen do while I was away at work? She's been very busy if she had time to destroy my house, read a book, and pleasure herself.

"You're mad at me because I lied to you?" I laugh again, not able to contain how ridiculous she's being.

"Yes," she hisses, completely serious as her face inches closer to mine. So close I could lean forward an inch and our lips would touch. I wouldn't even have to pretend it was a kiss. Just our angry words colliding.

"I hate to tell you, Siren, but lying is by far the least offensive of the crimes I plan on committing when it comes to you."

She stops breathing as she looks at my lips. She wants to kiss me too. I can tell in the way her breath hitches and her parted lips moisten.

But I'm too angry to let her have anything she wants. "I own you, Siren. You are mine. I can do whatever I want with you—including lie. But my lies should be the least of your worries."

Slap.

My head whips so hard to the side so fast I don't even

realize what just happened. For a second, I think that Julian or one of his men have attacked and punched me square in the jaw. But when I turn my head back to look at Siren, I realize the swing came from her. She's tiny; I have no idea how she was able to give her slap so much power.

It may be hard to believe, but I've been slapped by women before. None of which I completely deserved—until now. I earned every sting zipping through my jaw right now.

Siren is panting heavily underneath me. Her body is on alert, and if I say anything else stupid, she will slap me again with the full force of her petite body. She's definitely been taught how to defend herself. *From who?* I don't know. But that wasn't your average slap.

"Is that all you got? Because that pathetic tap won't stop me from getting what I want." I lower myself on top of her, until my body is pressing down on hers. Until my cock is resting against her stomach. Until she can barely breathe beneath me.

"Then rape me already! Get it over with! Stop playing games and get it over with!" she cries before her hand comes up again to slap me. I stop her automatically this time, more prepared than I was before.

I push her hands down into the armrests on either side of her. Now all she can move are her lips, as my head blocks any other movement. But her lips alone are dangerous enough.

"Do it. Rape me. I'd like to see you try. I'll cut off your dick before you have a chance."

I lean down until our lips are aligned but stop short of kissing. Her pink lips are taunting me in a way I can't resist, and her damn fucking smell is pulling me to her like a magnet. My raging hard-on is getting uncomfortable in my jeans. I didn't think this position through when I pinned her to the chair, because it's more torturous for me than her.

"Who says I want to rape you?" I say, my eyes searing. It's my biggest lie yet. Okay, I don't want to rape her, but I do want to fuck her—badly. I'm not sure I've ever wanted anything more.

Her eyes flicker down to where my erection gives me away. "He does."

I smirk. "Only a weak man lets his cock make the decisions. And I'm not a weak man. I'm a smart businessman who likes money."

She snickers. "You sure as hell don't look like any businessman I've ever met. And you aren't very smart with money if you are willing to drop thirty million on a woman when you could easily pick up some woman at a bar with your body."

"I am focused on my money, which is why I don't want to rape you. It's like driving a brand new car off the car lot. You would instantly lose your value if I was the one to break you in. As you said, I spent too much money on you to let that happen."

Her face drops into concern as she struggles carefully against my body. I'm so close she can barely move without our lips touching. And she won't give me that satisfaction.

"Then, what do you want from me, if not my body?"

"I want to sell you. We are going to Julian Reed's Friday night. He's inviting some of the richest men in the world. Men that would make the boys at the auction seem poor. I'm going to sell you and double my money."

Her mouth drops open, speechless.

All of my words are lies. I don't want to sell her; I want to protect her. And selling her to Julian Reed would be sentencing her to a life of torture. But she doesn't know that.

I need her to fear me. I need her obedient. Especially if we go to Julian's. I don't need him suspecting I haven't touched her yet.

"Now, slap me again, and I'll make sure you go to the most ruthless man instead of the one with the biggest pockets. Understand?"

She nods slowly.

"Good." Although, I'm not sure I like her so silent. Her body lies to me, I can feel it. There is no way she's actually attracted to me. No way her nipples are hardening in my direction. No way the scent of sex is growing. No way she is licking her lips because she wants me. When she speaks, she tells the truth. She's told me as much before. She hated it when I lied, probably because she's a horrible liar. I need to get her talking.

"How do you know Julian Reed?"

I expect her to pretend she doesn't. I expect her to at least attempt to lie first—she doesn't.

"No," she flat out says.

"No? I don't think you get how this works. I ask you a question, you answer."

"No."

I growl.

"You just admitted you wouldn't hurt me because you're selling me to another man. You won't damage me before you do that. So no, I'm the one with control now. And I'm not going to answer your questions."

"I have a better idea," I retort.

She blinks, waiting for me to speak, but she still thinks she holds all the power.

"You always tell the truth. That's what you told me before, when I bought you."

She shifts beneath me but doesn't confirm or deny the truth.

"And you hated it when I lied to you, which means for you, telling the truth is your most important value. Something you won't waver on easily."

Again, she doesn't speak.

I smirk. *I have her.*

"Fine, you don't want to answer my questions, you don't have to."

She grins, thinking she won.

"But there will be consequences to your silence."

She narrows her gaze at me but doesn't move. She can't; I'm still holding her down to prevent another inevitable slap.

"You either tell me the truth, or I'll commit a sin." I don't tell her what the sin will be, but the look in my eyes gives her a clue. I won't be the gentleman I'm used to being. I'll unleash the beast. And once I do, there is no going back.

13

SIREN

TELL ME THE TRUTH, or I'll commit a sin.

Those words are going to be the death of me someday.

This man is all about playing games, because it's the only way he can beat me. He wants ultimate control over me. He wants me to spill all of my secrets and willingly give him my body. *Not going to happen.*

We both stare back and forth, neither of us backing down.

I refuse to be scared of his silly game.

And he refuses to show me any emotion other than absolute stillness.

Zeke's hands are still on me, but he's not manhandling me the way I might expect him to. His body is pressed against mine as he sits on top of me, and his hands have mine pinned to the armrests, but he isn't exerting all of his physical strength over me. His presence alone would have me bolted in place. He's so intense, unmoving, like a rock that can't be swayed by anything, even the wind.

He's a man of steel, only speaking words when necessary —only applying force when he needs to. Because he knows the costs of exerting his physical prowess on others. And he only reserves that for the most serious situations.

I'm the first to move, squirming beneath his hard body. I feel his erection against my stomach. He doesn't try to hide his attraction to me. He displays it proudly. And as much as I want to make a snarky comment about him being turned on by me—I can't. Because it would be a lie to tease him for his attraction when I'm equally turned on.

My self-pleasure session earlier did nothing to squash this deep craving in my core that has now spread to the tips of my fingers and toes. Every nerve, muscle, and bone in my body is screaming—I want Zeke.

I want to tug on his man bun sitting on top of his head, until his hair falls gruffly to his shoulders, turning him into more beast than man. I want to feel his stubble against my thigh. I want to feel the power of his hands as he pushes inside of me with his impressive cock. I want to fight back, determined to ride him instead of letting him fuck me. I want him to tame me, convince me that having a man in my life is a good thing.

I want to lose all control and forget how horrible men are. How selfish, egotistical, assholes all men are. I want to forget about him buying me. I want to pretend our only interaction before today was when I saved him.

I want...

I swallow. *It doesn't matter what I want.*

My eyes drop back to Zeke, who hasn't moved and gives me no clue of his thoughts. But I know that he's thinking. Every move he makes is calculated, including when he is as still as a statue.

His silence is driving me mad. I want answers. *I need answers!* I need to know the man beneath the shield. So I can hurt him, demolish him, and be one step closer to freedom.

I shift again, pretending I want to get away from him, while accidentally thrusting my hips up into his erection.

His lip twitches. *He notices.* His body stills, except for his eyes. It's less than a second, but I see them roll with pleasure.

Why isn't he going to try and have me, then? He wants me this badly. Does he really want to sell me to Julian or one of Julian's friends?

"Truth or sin. What does that mean?" I finally ask.

Zeke looks down at my hands gripping the armrest. With an unspoken promise, he releases me. I expect him to be hesitant and wait for me to slap him again. But he doesn't. He trusts me. *How foolish of him.*

Zeke stands up and walks over to the far side of the room. He returns with a second wine glass and a bottle of wine. He fills his glass, then mine. This bottle is one of the last of his alcohol supply to survive my tornado. I destroyed or hid all the rest.

I take the glass from him; our fingers tingle when our hands brush. *Stupid body, always choosing the wrong men.*

Zeke takes a drink, and so do I. He has this unyielding power over me. I almost wish he'd speak. I can fight back word for word. I can use my snarky wit to knock him on his ass and put him on the defensive. But I can't fight back without him talking. I can't resist his pull. It's like gravity pulling me to him, commanding me to follow his unspoken words.

I clear my throat, trying to break free from the spell. "What do you mean?" I ask again.

He doesn't let my question or uncomfortableness speed

up his answers. He takes his time, drinking more of his wine as he waits me out.

I try to sit up taller in the chair while he stands over me. But it's no use. With his six foot five frame towering over me as I sit in the chair, I can't help but feel small.

Finally, he kneels in front of me. Reducing his power, but making me more uncomfortable now that we are eye to eye.

"Better?" he asks.

My mouth is dry. *How can he read me so easily?* I shake my head, trying to wash all feeling from my body.

He raises one eyebrow. "Hmm, well then make up your mind, Siren. Should I kneel or stand?"

"Sit...in a chair." *Like a normal person.*

He shakes his head slowly. "That wasn't one of the choices. Kneel or stand?"

My eyes flicker back and forth, trying to read his. "Kneel," I whisper.

He nods and continues to kneel.

Holy hell. Why is this big, muscular, powerful man kneeling in front of me? And why is it the sexiest thing I've ever seen?

He finishes his wine and sets it down on the end table next to me. He still hasn't answered my question.

Then he reaches for my wine glass. I let him take it. I don't need more alcohol in my system if I'm going to have a fighting chance against Zeke. He's not like other men. And that terrifies me. I don't know how to play him if he's constantly two steps ahead of me.

But when he reaches for the glass, he grabs my fingers too. He lifts the glass to his own lips and drinks. His eyes looking up at me as he drinks from the glass I'm holding.

I change my mind; *this* is the sexiest thing I've ever seen. It's such a simple move, but I can feel his touch, his breath all the way to my core. My toes tingle and my pussy drenches just from his lips being so close to my fingers. His hand is touching mine in a controlling but kind way.

I bite my lip, trying to keep from gasping and moaning while he drinks. When he finishes the last drop of my wine, he takes a deep inhale.

I think he's breathing in the wine, but the mischievous look on his face tells me otherwise.

"It appears that you have already sinned," he says.

I blink rapidly. *Can he still smell my cum on my fingers?* My cheeks heat at his accusation. I shouldn't be the least bit embarrassed; I'm a grown woman who can touch herself as much as she wants. I practically paraded naked around his house. I flashed his cameras, showed him how I came. I thought it would be a big fuck you, but right now, I think it's a big fuck me.

"How do I know?" he asks, asking my unspoken question out loud.

I nod.

He shakes his as he releases my hand. "This is how the game works. You want answers, you have to be willing to give everything. You have to risk the highest price in order to get the truth."

"Touching myself isn't a sin."

"Yes, it is—*to me.*"

I cock my head, not understanding.

"You belong to me, Siren. You. Are. Mine. You don't get to touch yourself without my permission. Your pussy belongs to me. Your pleasure belongs to me. You touched what is mine. To me, that's a sin."

His words infuriate me, and somehow also turn me on. No man has ever talked about owning my pussy or pleasure like that.

"You don't own me," I whisper—not terrified, but not strong enough to say the words so loudly. Not because I'm scared of Zeke, but because on some level, I want a man to lay claim to my body. I want to be controlled. I'm tired of having to do every-fucking-thing for myself. I want a man who can make me come better than I can.

Zeke leans forward until his mouth is against my ear. "No, Siren, maybe I don't. Because to truly own someone, the other person has to willingly give himself back. But soon, I will. Because you are on the verge of giving me everything."

He sits back. And once again, I'm left speechless.

"So, how does this silly game of yours work?" I ask, clearing my throat.

He sits back on his heels. "I ask you a question. You tell the truth. And if you don't want to answer, you have to let me commit a sin against you."

"And what about me? Do I get to ask a question? Do I get to commit a sin if you don't answer?"

"Yes," he answers, surprising the hell out of me. I assumed this would be one-sided. But this might be exactly what I need to be able to get my own answers.

"And if we choose to answer the question, how do we know we are both telling the truth?"

He lets out a breathy growl as if the question I asked is ridiculous. "We both know the answer to that."

I run my hand through my long hair, wishing Zeke would do the same—come unhinged a little, let his hair down, and stop controlling my every thought. But he doesn't. His hair stays high up on his head, locked away with a black scrunchie.

"You told me you can't lie. And I believe you."

"I can too lie...I um...fuck," I breathe, not even being able to lie about lying.

He smirks. "See? You can't lie."

Now it's my turn to growl.

He smiles in a charming, bright way—*fucking asshole.*

"Fine, but someday, I might figure out how to lie and how will you be able to hold me accountable?"

He leans forward again. "Because if you find a way to lie with your words, your body will betray you. Your cheeks will shade just the slightest darker pink. More blood will flow to your lips until they are as red as a poisoned apple. Your eyes will dilate. You'll fidget just the tiniest bit more. And your body will melt under my scrutiny."

As he speaks, everything he says happens to my body. *How can he control me that much?*

"And how will I know you aren't lying? You've already lied to me."

"And you figured out I was lying within an hour of me being gone."

"So? I don't expect our game to last an entire hour."

"I suspect you are a fast learner."

I laugh. "I'm really not. I'm the worst learner. It takes me forever to master a skill. I have to put in way more than my ten thousand hours to learn something. But once I master it, I never forget. I don't have to practice anymore." *Why the fuck am I telling him this much about myself?* I'm just willingly spilling all of my secrets.

His eyes widen at my admission.

I clamp my mouth shut to keep from admitting any more stupid secrets.

"I grew up in New Orleans. My mother is in prison; my father died when I was five. I worked as a mechanic for a few years in my early teens. I met my first girlfriend in college at the University of Texas. I studied biology, but never finished my degree."

My mouth slowly unclamps at each of his admissions—wow.

"Did I speak the truth?" he asks.

I think back to how he delivered each sentence. I close my eyes, trying to remember every syllable he spoke, the inflection, and any clues his body gave away. Most people would have said there were no clues—nothing to give away if he spoke the truth or not. He delivered his words with the same calm stillness he does everything else with.

No—he didn't tell the truth.

When he is speaking the truth, he is passionate about what he says, and his voice is husky and intoxicating. My body would follow any command he'd give. I could listen to Zeke talk all damn day.

His voice was still deep and sexy, but it was slightly different. If he spoke a command in that voice, I wouldn't have had to listen to his order unless I wanted to.

His body was more tense than still.

His eyes glazed over just a little, trying to hide the truth.

"You lied," I say.

"How did you know?"

I shake my head with a light smile. "I'm not telling you my secrets."

He narrows his eyes in a scowl, which only brightens my smile.

"Fine, don't tell me what my tells are. But you trust that you will be able to tell when I'm lying?"

"Yes."

"And if either of us is caught lying to the other, then he, or she, gets to commit the ultimate sin."

I swallow the lump down. I don't have to ask what he

means by 'ultimate sin.' There is one universal sin that all people, animals, and culture believe is the worst—murder. If I lie, and he catches me, then he will kill me. If he lies, I kill him.

These are the ultimate stakes. The highest bet either of us can put on the table. But we both want each other's secrets.

Zeke wants to know about my relationship with Julian, while I need Zeke's secrets to use against him and free myself.

We are both willing to risk everything for the truth.

I nod, silently agreeing to his terms.

Most men would want to hear my words, not Zeke. All forms of communication are equal in his book.

"We can only play max once a day," Zeke says.

I agree. I don't like endless prodding and questions about my life.

"Follow up questions have to be asked the next day."

I nod.

"And you don't have to reveal anything other than the basic answer to the question. Elaboration happens with further questions."

Again I nod, agreeing. I will have to be careful with how I ask my questions to get the most answers from Zeke, while trying to keep my big mouth shut. Zeke is clearly used to keeping his answers simple, so I doubt I'll get more than one sentence. He might even try to answer me with a single word if I'm not careful.

"You first," I say, assuming he will ask me about Julian, and I'm not sure if I'll answer or choose sin. I don't want to talk about Julian, but I don't want to let Zeke commit a sin against me. He could choose anything from kissing to raping me—anything but killing me.

And I have no idea what question I'll ask him.

Zeke licks his lips, and my eyes are glued to his sensual mouth and rough five o'clock shadow darkening his square jaw.

"Do you find me attractive?" Zeke asks.

"What?" I gape.

He reaches up to his head, and pulls the scrunchie from his head and puts it on his wrist. His hair falls down, making him look like the human prince from Beauty and the Beast.

I can't blink, I can't breathe, I can't speak. My body is beyond attracted to him. He already knows that. I may hate how my body reacts to his, but it's not something he has to ask me to know it to be true. If this is the question he's asking me, it's a waste of a question.

He waits, patiently, still kneeling in front of me. "What will it be? Answer the question truthfully, or do I get to commit a sin against you?"

"The sinning part—can be anything you choose?"

He nods, his eyes like fire ready to burn me the second I refuse to answer the question. "Anything except murder."

I nod. I was right in my understanding of what a sin could be. And I can't believe I fell for his twisted game. He likes torturing me before he beats and rapes me. It's more fun to think it's my fault he's hurting me than to just fucking do it himself—*fucking coward.*

This is the easiest question, but also the hardest to admit. We both already know the truth, but I know nodding won't be enough this time. He wants me to verbalize my feelings. Whether I answer or not, he wins. He either gets me to admit my attraction, which he will use against me, or he gets to rape me.

I grit my teeth in anger at his ridiculous question. He doesn't care about Julian or getting honest answers from me.

He just enjoys the slow torture. I won't let him win. He doesn't get to hurt me tonight. I won't let him. I'll answer him. Words and teasing won't hurt me.

"Yes," I answer, refusing to give Zeke more than a single syllable answer. Luckily, it's enough to please him.

His face darkens, and I can tell he's thinking about all the dirty things he wants to do to me.

"Your turn," he says.

I think for a moment through my red, angry cheeks and grinding teeth. I'm not going to waste my question like Zeke did. Although, from the amount of rage I'm now experiencing, he didn't waste his question. He got me riled up and unfocused.

"Do you enjoy taking women as your slave?" I spit out in anger. *Yes, my question sucks and doesn't get me any real answers.* But I'm pissed. I want him to admit he's a monster, just like I had to admit I find him attractive.

I tap my fingers hard against the soft fabric of the armrests, wishing my nails could make an annoying tapping sound to unnerve him. I glare at Zeke, demanding an answer. A simple yes will satisfy me, just as I answered him.

"Sin."

I blink rapidly. *Wait...what?*

"I won't answer your question. I choose sin."

I'm speechless. I gave him an easy question, and rather than answer me truthfully, he'd rather let me commit a sin against him. I search his eyes to see if he set a trap, but I don't find any there.

My wheels turn, trying to come up with the perfect sin to inflict upon him. After a few moments, I grin slyly when I find the right one. Now to figure out if Zeke will keep to his word and take my wrath.

14

ZEKE

WHY DIDN'T I ask her about Julian? Why didn't I ask the most important question?

I know why. Once I get an answer, this will end. She will go free. She will no longer be mine. Our time together will be over.

I don't know how I know exactly, but I know. The question is too important. The truth she is hiding is too big. I can see it in her surprised eyes when I didn't ask the obvious question. By not asking, I got more information about how important the answer is than if I had asked. Sure, I might have gotten to commit a sin if she wasn't ready to share the answer with me. But once I start committing sins, I won't be able to stop—not with Siren.

Why did I choose sin instead of answering her question?

Because I had no choice—I either lie or tell her the truth. And even though she thought her question was an easy one, it wasn't. I'm not the man she thinks I am. I didn't want to buy her like I would a car, but I had no choice.

Just like I have no choice but to choose sin instead of

truth. I can't tell her the truth, and she would know if I lied —so sin it is.

"What is your sin?" I ask, still kneeling between her legs, staring eye to eye with her. When I first knelt in front of her, it was to get her to trust me; now, it's tempting me in ways I never imagined. Being so close to her and not being able to touch her, not being able to rip her sweatpants off and devour her sweet pussy—*kneeling was definitely a mistake.*

"Hmm," her lips purse as she contemplates her decision. I know she is going to push my limits even further. She knows she is my weakness, and for some reason, I'm not letting myself have her. The lie I told was that I'm going to sell her to make a profit as long as she is untouched. But I'm not sure she bought that lie.

Siren thinks I'm ruthless and cruel, but I'll protect her with my life. I've already moved her into the very limited circle of people who I would defend no matter the cost.

Her eyes darken as they go back in forth in search of finding something in my eyes. But I'm as blank as a sheet of paper. I won't yield any truths outside the game.

"I'm going to need some real clothes," she says.

"No, that's not part of the deal. You get what I decide to give you."

She frowns and folds her arms over her chest, lifting her legs up into the seat, trying to get as far away from me as possible.

"I knew you were a liar and would go back on our deal."

"I'm not going back on our deal. You can commit any sin you want. I just don't have to fund it or supply you with clothes or anything you need to commit the sin."

She shakes her head. "I have nothing. I own nothing. You've given me nothing! How am I supposed to commit a sin when I have nothing to work with?"

I shrug. "That's not my problem."

She pouts for a second, then says, "I can use anything I find? Anything I own or lay claim to in order to commit my sin?"

I narrow my eyes and lean forward, not sure where she is going with this. "Yes."

She hops over the side of the armrest and then starts running through the house.

She's going to be the death of me; I can feel it.

A second later, I chase after her. I'm fast, but due to my height and weight, I'm not as nimble as she is. She can hop over and dart around the various pieces of broken glass and furniture before I even see them.

She's out the front door before I get to the foyer. But I'm out the door in two giant leaps. She's running for my truck —the driver's side. My keys are still in my pocket; she can't start the truck. *Right?* But I don't stop to recall if the keys are still in my pocket or if I accidentally left them in the truck.

I run to the passenger side.

Siren is sitting on the driver's side. Her hands are on the wheel, and her seatbelt is already fastened.

"And where do you think you are going without the keys?" I smirk.

She bites her lip, trying to hide her mischievous grin. "I'm not going anywhere without the keys. Thanks for bringing them."

And with that, she starts the truck and puts her foot on the gas, flooring it.

Damn it, I'm a fucking idiot!

I'm used to older trucks, the kind where you have to put the key into the ignition to start it. But even though this truck has already been beaten to death by the previous owner, it has a key fob. You don't need to put it into the ignition, but I usually do out of habit. I consider jumping out of the truck, so the key is no longer in the vehicle. But I'm not sure removing the key fob from the car at this point will even shut the truck off. She could drive anywhere. She could get free.

It could be a good thing...unless Julian finds her.

I grab for my seatbelt instead and buckle myself in as she drives dangerously fast through Julian's compound.

"Where are we going?" I ask.

She smirks. "This is my choice—my sin. And I'm not telling yet. You'll just have to wait and see."

I silently punish myself for coming up with this game. I thought it would get Siren to trust me enough to spill her secrets. And it might over time, but right now, all I've accomplished is cursing her and myself to hell.

Siren takes a hard left turn off Julian's property onto the main gravel and sand road. My body gets thrown into the window as she turns.

"Slow the fuck down," I curse under my breath.

"Fucking hypocrite," she chuckles back.

"What did you just say?"

She turns toward me, her eyes no longer on the road as she drives faster. "You heard me."

I growl and sit back in my seat, my hand instinctively grabbing the door handle as she takes another sharp turn too fast. *She's right; I'm a hypocrite.* I drove fast just to get her under my control. She's just doing the same thing.

But one way or another, I'm going to be the one driving the truck home. Whether her ass is in it or not.

Siren flicks on the radio to fill the silence. She bobs her head to the music and mouths the words along to the song. But she doesn't sing. I haven't heard her sing since the night she saved me. *Maybe I imagined it?* I don't know how much of what I remember is real or made up. But after spending more time with Siren, I don't think I will ever forget a single second of my time with her.

I wait for her to start singing along, but she doesn't.

Finally, she stops in one of the local towns, parking the car illegally in front of one of the storefronts.

"What are you doing?" I ask, my heart still racing from the death-defying ride over here.

She unbuckles her seatbelt happily, like a teenager about to go shopping with their father's credit card at the mall.

"Getting new clothes," she says, before swinging her door open.

"With what money?" I ask as I jump out of the truck to go after her. It's only then that I realize my wallet is missing.

How the hell did she pull that off?

I don't have a clue. She must have been a thief in a previous life. I really need to ask questions that will give me some actual answers about who Siren is.

She skips up and down all bubbly as she heads into the first department store. I follow and corner her before she can use my money to buy some clothes. My body presence alone corners her between two racks of clothes.

"Give me back my wallet."

She tosses it to me. And then darts under my arm.

Wait...that was too easy.

She struts across the store and starts talking to one of the employees. And then she flashes me one of her *I'm going to kick your ass one day* smiles and hands the woman my credit card.

I'm searing. I'm sure actual fumes are coming out of my ears. She thinks these games are going to protect her. Her strategy is to keep her secrets by torturing me so I'll want to surrender to her. *Think again.* She has no idea who she is messing with. I'm going to wreck her.

———

AFTER SIREN'S little shopping spree that included buying half a dozen jeans, a couple of heels, and twenty designer shirts, she's finished spending my money. We are back in the truck, this time with me in the driver's seat and her in the passenger seat.

"Time to go home," I say.

She shakes her head. "You think that was my sin?"

I frown. "Yes, you just spent thousands of dollars on clothes. I think that counts as a sin."

She laughs. "Not even close." She kicks her feet up on my dashboard. "We are going to the bar on seventh street. That is where I'll complete my sin."

I sigh. I'm tired, and I don't feel like fighting her. I need her to trust me. And I need this night to be over. Tomorrow I have more important things to deal with—mainly Julian.

So that's how I end up driving Siren to a bar.

She practically sprints out of the car the second I stop, assuming I'm going to try and stop her after I drove her all the way here—she has a lot to learn about me.

I take my time getting out of the truck, after making sure I have my wallet with all my credit cards.

I walk into the crowded bar, taking in its steely decorations, making it look more like a dance club than a bar. It feels like every tourist on the island is packed in this place.

I find Siren at the end of the bar already flirting with a man, clearly ordering her a drink.

I walk up behind her. I know she can feel me behind her because goosebumps have risen on her arms.

She's wearing jeans, heels, and some black strapless shirt that makes her toned shoulders easy for my teeth to sink into. I've never been into biting during sex, but her shoulders taunt me in a way that makes me want to try sinking my teeth into her. Pleasurably watching tiny drops of blood drip off those sexy shoulders would ease the fury she boils inside me.

She doesn't turn around, and I don't need her to in order to get my message across.

I lean down close to her neck. I don't have to lean down much now that she is wearing heels—heels I'm secretly happy she bought because they are sexy as hell.

"If you ask anyone in here for help, if you try to run, if you tell anyone the truth...there will be consequences."

She shivers at my throaty words.

"But I hope you do try to run, because I enjoy chasing. And I'll enjoy inflicting the punishment even more."

She stops breathing as my words sink in.

My threats are real. I don't want her to run. Julian is too infatuated with her. He would find her, rape her, and sell her. Threatening and inflicting consequences is the only way to show how serious I am about protecting her.

I walk away to go order a drink and sit in one of the booths to wait for her sin. I'm already afraid I know what it's going to be...and I'm not sure my restraint is prepared for what she's about to do.

15

SIREN

I've enjoyed teasing Zeke all night.

I didn't think I'd enjoy driving Zeke's big, worn-down truck, but I was wrong. I understand now the thrill of feeling power over the world when you drive it. The truck drives like it doesn't give a fuck that it's run-down and should be scrapped for metal. It drives like it owns the road, and anyone in its way needs to get the fuck out.

I get it; I'm the same as the truck. A little rough around the edges, but more powerful than anyone suspects at first glance. And I loved using that power to make Zeke regret ever buying me.

When I stole his wallet, the look of shock on his beautifully sculpted face will stay with me forever. I don't know what he thought of the move—if I had practiced stealing before or if I got lucky. And I'll never tell him the truth.

I've had a fun night—until Zeke breathed down my neck. Until his words held promises and threats of what would happen if I ran. He doesn't know I have no intention of running. He may suspect I'm scared of Julian, but he doesn't know why. He doesn't know Julian would hunt me to the ends of the earth without Zeke's protection.

But Zeke's heated threat almost makes me want to run, just so he will chase me. Just so he can *punish me.*

I don't run, though. Instead, I let the handsome man I found the second I walked into the bar order me a shot of tequila. We both take the shot. Then I stroke the stranger's strong forearm, flash him a bright smile, and wink before sauntering off.

I felt Zeke's gaze on me the entire time, but if he thinks flirting with a stranger at the bar is the sin I plan on committing against him tonight, he's in for a surprise.

I strut across the room to the dance floor, making eye contact with a man dancing seductively with a woman.

My turn—my eyes and body say.

The man's gaze finds me immediately. What can I say, I know how to attract men to me like a moth to a flame. I will burn every single man who thinks he has a claim to me.

I scrape my teeth over my bottom lip and bat my eyelashes at him, then I wait. He will ditch his date for me.

And right on cue, he does. The woman yells and scowls at the man, but he isn't listening anymore. I have him thoroughly under my spell.

"Dance with me," he says.

I crook my finger under his chin. "Let's see if you can keep up."

I don't introduce myself or ask for his name. This isn't serious. This is about sex, even if we never get to the physical act. We will dance, and it will be as close to sex as you can get with your clothes still on.

I grab his neck, he grabs my hips, and then we are moving, grinding on each other through the thick crowd of people. We only need a second to learn each other's style.

And then we are effortlessly moving across the floor—our bodies dancing on top of each other. I push; he pulls. The sexual tension between us is palpable. If I had control over my life right now, we'd end up in the closest hotel room.

Instead, this is all I get.

I give the man everything I have while dancing with him. I don't search to see if Zeke can see me. If he's smart, he will pull out his phone and get buried in it, instead of watching me.

I know Zeke wants me, but for some reason, he isn't going to touch me until he decides if he wants me more than he wants to sell me to Julian. I'm about to make that decision so much harder for him.

Suddenly, I feel like I have more eyes on me. The room has circled around me, and I know that Zeke is watching.

Good. I'm about to murder his heart.

The dance ends, and I pull the hot man I'm using flush to my body. Our mouths pant over each other, but I don't kiss him. And I don't let him kiss me.

The crowd claps and hollers, cheering us on—wanting another dance.

But I have a better idea to give them a full show.

While my dance partner inches closer to grabbing my ass, I look over his shoulders and find the DJ behind him.

I crook my finger at him, and he runs toward me.

"Can I use the mic, and can you play 'Truth Hurts' by Lizzo?" I ask.

"You can have whatever you want," he says with a wink.

I look back to my dance partner. "Can you sing?"

He chuckles. "They don't care if I sing. But I can show you off."

"Good enough."

The DJ returns with the microphone, and the song I requested starts.

My hot dance partner spins me around, and I start singing with him dancing around me.

As I sing, the room quiets. I've always been a good singer. I've sung numerous times in the shower or car, but never publicly. But I don't doubt the power of my voice.

The man holds me in his arms, swinging our hips together as I belt out the song.

My eyes find Zeke's. He's sitting at a round table directly across from me. The crowd has parted, and Zeke has the perfect view of me. So I sing for him. I let him know he will never have me. I will never be his. And I can have any man in this room.

I up my game, teasing the man holding me and walking over and touching or rubbing against every other man in the room. But it's not enough. I want my sin to hurt Zeke.

So I turn to my dance partner, rip off his shirt to the hoop and hollers of every female in the room. And then I kiss down his chest as I sing before rubbing my ass on his hard-on.

The song ends, and I'm covered in sweat and exhilaration. My dance partner leans down to kiss me, but I move at the last second, and his kiss falls to my shoulder. My eyes lock with Zeke.

I could let him kiss me, *but I didn't.*

I could let him fuck me, *but I won't.*

As long as you behave, this is as far as I will go. I'll never make you imagine me with another man unless you give me reason to.

"Thank you for the dance," I say to my partner before strutting over to Zeke.

Zeke watches me carefully and finishes his drink before waving the hot waitress over.

She smiles at him brightly while bending over so he can see down her blouse as she takes his order. But he doesn't look; his gaze is still on me. And I can see the agitation in his eyes at having to watch me dance all over a shirtless man, and knowing that every man in the room wants me—*I can choose any of them.*

My sin worked; he's pissed.

But then Zeke grabs the waitress and dips her over his lap. She laughs hysterically as he whispers something close to her lips. She nods enthusiastically at his words.

And then he leans down and kisses her, with his eyes still locked on mine. He asked if he could kiss her. So he is capable of asking a woman for permission before he takes what he wants. He just won't do that with me.

I thought my flirting without crossing the line was a good sin. I was wrong—Zeke's sin is better. He damaged me worse than I injured him, and it isn't even his turn to sin. I don't think I can handle what he will do when it is.

16

ZEKE

THE SECOND MY lips touch the waitress's lips, I know it's a mistake. I thought the kiss would hurt Siren, pay her back for all the flirting, dancing, and rubbing on that man she did. But the kiss feels wrong in every way.

I asked the waitress if I could kiss her before I did it. I'm not the kind of man who takes something from a woman without asking before. But Siren saw me ask—and she's pissed. Because she thinks I would never ask before I took from her.

As my lips press against the waitress's thin, pink lips, I feel awful. This kiss is good, simple, not too wet. When I shove my tongue between her lips, I taste the sweet wine she must be sipping between customers behind the bar. It's pleasant and awful.

I'm not the kind of man who feels a rush of emotions with a kiss. I've never fallen hard for a woman I've been intimate with before. Never experienced that head over heels feeling for another woman. And I sure as hell don't feel that now kissing Samantha—at least that's what her name tag says. In fact, I feel the opposite. I feel regret, remorse, and stupidity.

I should not have kissed her.

I should not have taunted Siren.

I thought that I would pay her back for hurting me with her sin. But instead, my move backfired, and I ended up damaging myself more.

Siren's face full of disappointment and anger is like a shock to the heart. I didn't realize how much I cared about what Siren thought of me until now.

I thought the kiss would make me stop thinking about Siren. I would realize I just needed to get laid to forget about her. But the kiss made my obsession for Siren worse and did nothing to quell my desire for her. It just showed me how a kiss from any other woman isn't enough.

I want Siren.

I want to kiss her.

I want her in my bed.

I want her writhing underneath me as I thrust into her.

I want her riding my cock on top of me as she digs her nails into my chest.

I want...fuck, I can't even think it. Because I want so much more than just a good fuck when it comes to Siren.

When Siren committed her sin against me, I thought I was going to lose my mind. But not out of jealousy like she wanted me to feel. Sure, I wanted to be the one she was dancing all over. I wanted to be the man whose cock she rubbed with her curvy ass. But watching her move, listening to her sing, seeing her confidence as she took control of the entire room—I could search a lifetime and never find a woman like her.

I always knew I'd need a strong woman if I were to ever settle down. My lifestyle requires a woman who can hold her own—a powerful woman who doesn't put up with any man's shit.

Siren is that woman.

And I'm torn between setting her free and finding a way to make her mine, for real.

I know she wants my body. She's made that clear. But she could never love the man beneath the hard exterior. Because unlike her, I commit sins every day. I steal, beat, and murder. I'll even end up selling women if it comes down to it, because I'm only truly loyal to a small handful.

And she will never get past any of that. I could bring her chocolates and flowers every day of her life. I could court her and take her to fancy dinners, dancing, and movies. None of that would matter. She's already seen the worse part of my heart. She will never see me as anything other than cruel.

But it doesn't stop my cock from hardening or my heart from hoping she was brought into my life for something more than just saving me in the ocean.

"I get off in an hour. We could get a room at the hotel down the street," the waitress says, still sitting in my lap with her hands around my neck.

Shit, I'd completely forgotten about her.

"Sorry, a work thing came up. Thanks for the kiss." I try to smile and give her my best apologetic beam, but from the hurt look on her face, she thinks I'm the kind of man who will kiss a woman and then dump her when he finds a better-looking woman to take home. And she's right.

She stands but turns at the last minute, and I already know where she's headed with her movements. She's going to slap me.

But she's not as fast as Siren. She's not practiced the

movement enough. So I grab her wrist before she even winds back to slap me.

She frowns, glaring at me like I'm the devil. If she only knew how true her thoughts were.

I dig into my wallet and pull out a couple of twenties. I hand them to her. "Thank you for the drinks."

At first, I think she's going to reject the money. But she grabs it hastily and shoves the wad into her bra before stomping off.

Siren laughs, like what she witnessed was the funniest shit she's ever seen—me getting told off and almost slapped by a waitress. But I see past her light chuckles. She's hurt—I hurt her with that kiss. It was my intention, but seeing the pain behind her eyes makes me regret my decision even more.

Finally, she stops laughing and walks over to me. "I thought I was the only one who got to sin tonight."

"You telling me that kiss hurt you? Because that would mean you are jealous of a waitress. It would mean you want me to kiss you. I know you find me attractive, but I thought you thought more highly of yourself." *I'm such an asshole.*

This time Siren doesn't take my bait. She just walks away.

We walk toward my truck in silence.

"Any chance you want to let me go?" she asks, her voice heavy. She doesn't look up at me. She just stops next to the passenger door like she's ready to accept her fate, but she'd rather run.

"Never," I answer honestly. *I never want to let her go.*

She sucks in a deep breath, and I swear I see tears in her eyes. Siren doesn't strike me as the type that cries often. So the fact that this moment is when the tears start surprises me.

Finally, she nods and then climbs into the passenger side. Without fighting me about who is driving.

I take my time climbing into the driver's side, hoping she will have stopped sobbing by the time I climb in.

She hasn't—her crying has gotten worse. Tears are pouring out of her eyes, and her voice is wailing in pain.

What's happening?

I don't understand why she's crying so much or in so much pain. But the fact that I can't ask—the fact that I can't touch her, can't console her, hurts me worse than watching her dance with that man. It hurts worse than watching her kiss another man. It hurts worse than knowing she's fucked another man.

It hurts, seeing her in this much anguish. It hurts so much that I almost want to let her go. This is the worst sin she could ever commit, hurting and not letting me do a damn thing to help her. This sin destroys me. This sin will be my undoing.

17

———

SIREN

My tears break him.

I didn't expect them to. I've just had so much emotion floating through my body I needed a release. I promised myself I would stop as soon as Zeke got into the truck.

But as soon as I saw his face, felt his nervous energy, and saw him fidgeting with the steering wheel and keys like it was his first time driving, I knew the tears just became my sin, not the flirting and dancing.

For a second, I thought I should have kissed my dance partner, because that jealousy would have hurt Zeke the most. Turns out, jealousy barely registers on his radar.

But seeing me in pain, that hurts him.

Huh.

Is that why he hasn't raped me despite wanting to? He's torn between what he wants and not being able to handle seeing me in pain?

I keep crying, and the pain deepens on his face—so I cry harder, seeing how far I can take it before he completely shatters. I need to know his limits. It's the only way to destroy him.

154

My sobbing turns to heartbreaking wails, the kind women use only after the worst happens to them—the loss of a spouse or child. But my cries aren't acting. I'm not lying with my howls. Everything I'm letting out is exactly how I feel.

I'm trapped, and I've lost everything and everyone important to me. Even if Zeke lets me go, I still won't get back what I lost. I'll never be whole again.

Suddenly, the truck stops. My eyes are red with tears blanketing my vision, so I can't tell if we are back at Zeke's house or if he stopped somewhere else.

He unbuckles and climbs out. I reach over for my seatbelt and fidget with it until I finally get it to unlatch.

Zeke opens the door before I'm finished. He doesn't say a word. He doesn't tell me to stop. He doesn't comfort me with his body, even though his presence does strange things to mine—excites and soothes.

I move to climb out, but his body blocks me.

"What?" I ask, as the tears continue to fall.

He doesn't answer with words. Instead, I'm lifted up in the air and flipped over his shoulder until my face is staring right at his glorious ass.

My sobs are stifled as it's hard enough to breathe flipped over like this, let alone cry.

Zeke carries me like a caveman away from the truck. I try to lift my head up to see where we are, but all I can see is his ass and then eventually the sand below his feet. Then I hear the crashing of waves.

Why are we on the beach?

The waves get closer, and I realize what Zeke is planning on doing.

I fist my hands and start pummeling his back with my fists.

"Don't. You. Dare," I say firmly between hiccuping sobs.

He doesn't speak or stop walking.

I watch the bottom half of his jeans get swallowed up by the waves. And then I'm being flung onto my back into the cool water.

I stay under the water longer than I need to. I love the water. I used to want to be a mermaid when I grew up. It took until I was a teenager to realize mermaids weren't real. I couldn't spend my life swimming in the water, rescuing dolphins, and saving sea creatures. I had to grow up and get a real job.

But sometimes, when I'm all alone in the water, I pretend my life is different. I pretend I'm just a mermaid, living her best life as a magical creature that won't let anyone hurt her.

I close my eyes as I come up out of the water. My heels somehow get washed from my feet, so my bare toes touch the smooth sand that feels like home. My hair covers my face, so I flip it back as I gasp in a deep breath, and the tears stop.

Despite hating that Zeke just threw me in the water, it did the trick. The water is where I feel alive and safe. There is no way I could cry right now, even if I wanted to.

I find Zeke's gaze on me.

"Enough," he says.

That one word vibrates through my body. And I feel it in all the ways he meant it—as a command and a question. He wants me to stop hurting, yet he's also asking if I've had enough. If I'm over whatever was hurting me because he can't handle my pain anymore.

And he can't be gentle with how he helps me get over my pain. Surprisingly, I don't want him to be. I want someone who knows when I'm hurting and puts an end to it abruptly.

I've never had a man care enough about me to do something about my pain, even in this unconventional way.

Zeke is now standing waist-deep in the water a foot from me. The waves wash up again, striking me in the back and Zeke in the chest, but it doesn't stop the intense connection we share. We aren't touching, yet in the water, I feel him. *All of him.* I feel his pain. It's a pain I don't understand. He's a powerful man with more money than sense. *What could he be possibly be hurting about?*

But it's there—his heart is bleeding as badly as mine is.

We stand there for another minute. Both giving the ocean everything we can never give to each other. Our pain. Our secrets. Our *truths.*

And when everything has been spilled, I nod.

Zeke turns with the nod and starts walking to the truck. He doesn't wait for me to follow. I could run. I could swim into the ocean, and he would never catch me. But I don't because now I'm curious about the man. The only man who has ever shown that he cares about my pain.

That man also happens to be my current owner, who might sell me on Friday. And I'm more confused than ever about who he is. *What kind of man is Zeke?*

We both climb into the truck soaking wet. I've lost both shoes and sand clings to my brand new jeans.

Zeke again doesn't look or speak to me as we drive. But I squirm a little, hating that I'm getting saltwater and sand all over his car.

"Don't worry about it. I'll have you clean it out tomorrow," Zeke says, with—*wait, is that a grin?*

I try to hide back my own smile, but I can't. I don't know how I went from pissed, to crying, to smiling in a matter of minutes, but I did. Zeke did that.

"I'm not your maid. I think you have enough money to hire someone to clean your car."

He raises an eyebrow. "But then I wouldn't get to see you in a slutty maid outfit."

I shake my head. "That is never happening."

"We'll see," he whispers.

Yes, we will see—and it's not happening.

As we drive past Julian's house, the joking moment we had before turns serious. My fear returns at just the sight of his property. Today is Wednesday. That means I only have one more day to convince Zeke not to bring me to that house. One more day to convince him not to sell me. One more day to put an end to all of this.

As I climb into Zeke's bed after showering, I know one day won't be enough.

18

ZEKE

I STILL DON'T UNDERSTAND what happened yesterday. How did I go from being pissed and hurt, to wanting to take away all of her pain?

Siren is a strong woman, but she's still a woman—still human. I forgot that because she always acts like a super-hero. She acts tough and resilient, like nothing could ever hurt her.

But last night, I learned she hurts just like all the rest of us; she just hides it better until the dam finally ruptures. And last night it burst.

How stupid was I to bring her to the water? I knew it would help her. I knew it would stop her tears. But it also sharpened our connection to each other. She learned things about me last night she shouldn't have. She learned I have a soft spot for her; I'm not as cruel as she thought. Which means I'm going to have an even harder time controlling her. An even a harder time keeping her safe.

I open my eyes, and instead of staring up at my white ceiling, I see Siren straddling my body—and what a sight she is. Even with her messy hair and sleepy eyes, I want her.

I could get used to waking up this way every morning. Yet, I don't think she's straddling me because she wants a quickie before I go to work. She wants something.

I grumble and roll my eyes. "What do you want?"

"A rematch."

I sigh. "A rematch?"

"Yes, I want another game of truth or sin tonight."

"Fine," I rub my eyes and then stretch my arms up over my head. I expect her to jump off me now that she's gotten what she wants, but she doesn't. She continues to straddle my waist, and if she moves a few inches lower, she will be greeted by a particular part of my body that would be very happy to get better acquainted with her pussy. She's wearing a layer of shorts and panties, but that barely separates us.

"Anything else?" I ask, rubbing my head. *I think I'm getting a headache from her.*

She grins brightly. "You aren't a morning person, are you?"

I growl, and she finally jumps off me. "No, I'm not. So I suggest you remember that before you wake me up like that again."

I get out of bed and pull on my jeans. I showered last night, so I don't bother today before I head into work. I have to meet Oscar today.

"Going to work?" she asks, her voice hesitant.

I nod, as I pull on a white T-shirt run my hand through my long hair, before pulling it up into a man bun.

"Are you going to lock me in a room again?" she snickers.

"Nope, you already learned that trick."

"But you are going to leave me here, alone?"

I turn toward her, raising an eyebrow. "Why shouldn't I? You already destroyed everything in my house. There is nothing left for you to damage."

She frowns. "Aren't you worried I will run?"

"Are you going to run?"

She doesn't answer.

I sigh. "No, I'm not worried. For one, I live too close to Julian's property. He has cameras everywhere. He would see you run. He would chase after you and only return you to me after he's had his turn with you. You already seem to know that, though, so I know you won't run."

She pulls the covers up over her body, immediately changing her demeanor when I talk about Julian.

I finish gathering my wallet and keys—not worried at all that she will still be here when I return. But I pause at the door, because I don't want a repeat of yesterday.

"I'm renting this place from Julian. And he sees everything that goes on in his house," I say, eyeing the camera in the door.

Siren's eyes go wide. I hacked the camera last night when I couldn't sleep to see what she did yesterday when I was gone. The sight of her pleasuring herself drove me insane. I deleted the footage, hoping Julian or his guards hadn't seen it yet. It was a risky move; Julian could notice my hack and the deleted footage. But I couldn't stand for him to see Siren like that.

I don't tell her that, though. Maybe it will get her to behave today to know Julian is watching her, not just me.

"And if you get bored, you can always start cleaning up the mess you made yesterday."

She snaps back to life. "You aren't going to hire someone to clean up and get you new furniture?"

I shake my head. "I'm really not. Why would I when you would just destroy it again?"

She pauses. She doesn't have a smart retort for that.

"Have a good day, Siren." And then I'm gone to go meet

Oscar and hope I can find a way out of the mess I've found myself in.

———

OSCAR SMILES at me as I pull up at the warehouse where he holds the women. The same warehouse Siren was held in just a few days ago. It makes my stomach flip to think about it.

Siren deserves so much better. She deserves to live the life she wants. She deserves to be happy with a man who can give her everything. She deserves to have the big house and two-point-five kids with a dog, if that's what she desires. I don't even know her well enough to know what she wants.

Is she a dog or a cat person?

Does she want kids? How many?

What was her job before she was captured? Does she want to return to that career or start something new?

Where does she want to live?

Does she want to get married?

No, none of those questions matter. Because I will never be the man to give her any of those things. There are only a few questions that actually matter. *What is her relationship to Julian? And where does she want me to drop her off?*

"Zeke? Are you listening?" Oscar asks.

"Yes, sir." *Fuck, now I'm calling Oscar 'sir.'*

"Good. Follow me."

I follow Oscar back into the depths of hell. I have to force my legs to follow him instead of running back to my truck and getting the fuck out of here.

But once inside the warehouse, there is a new stillness in the air. I don't hear the heavy breaths of the women afraid to breathe, let alone move. I don't hear the hustle and bustle of his men moving supplies around. It's almost eerily quiet.

Oscar notices my change in expression. "Our other shipper picked up the women last night." He grins. "It's a great feeling to know all my hard work paid off, and the money has hit my bank account."

I squeeze my teeth down to keep from chewing him out before clobbering him into the ground with my fists. I'm grinding my molars so hard I'm sure I've rubbed off a layer of enamel, and Oscar can hear the sound of my teeth destroying each other. But if he notices, he doesn't react. He just continues to talk about the women he sold like they were cattle.

I need to get out of here. "When will you have a shipment for us?"

He smiles. "Two weeks."

Shit.

That's not enough time for me to form a plan on how to save them. That's barely enough time to make a real plan to try and sell them.

I'm screwed.

And so are the women he's about to take.

My soul will forever be tarnished. There is no forgiveness for men who sell people. I'll be banished to eternal damnation. I won't be able to look at myself in the mirror. And I sure as hell won't be worthy of a woman like Siren, even to kiss her. My lips alone would burn her like fire. She's pure; I'm evil.

"How many?" I ask, needing as much information as possible.

"We should be able to do two-hundred easily."

Fuck, it's worse than I thought. Two hundred women. I'm

having a hard enough time saving one woman; there is no way I can save two hundred.

————

I slam the door as I return to the house. I need a drink—no, I need six. This is hopeless. There is nothing I can do. I don't have the money to buy two hundred women while secretly letting them all go free—no one does.

Fuck, I'm spineless. I should be going into Oscar's warehouse guns blazing, trying to kill every man who works for him. That's the only way to save the women.

I'd have to kill Julian too, but he's been very careful. He has more men working for him than he lets on. If I attack him, I need to know every single one of his men, or I'll spend my life running and looking over my shoulder.

It's too late, anyway. Most of Oscar's men are already out somewhere kidnapping women. I don't know who they are or how to stop them. In two weeks, the women will be mine. And I'm still clueless as to what I'm supposed to do.

"You're back," Siren says, leaning against the door of the kitchen as she holds a high-ball glass filled with amber liquid.

"Where did you get that?"

She grins. "I made sure not to break all of your glasses and liquor."

I walk to her.

She doesn't retreat. She stands her ground.

I stop inches from her. So close, yet so far. I take in a deep breath. I can't even smell the liquor. All I smell is her— a fresh, citrus, watery scent.

She wags her finger in front of me. "You aren't getting any of this. This has to last me the entire time I'm here, since you refuse to restock the liquor cabinet. I'm not sharing."

"You destroyed my liquor and glasses! And most of my fucking house! I shouldn't be the one to replace any of it, you should."

She bites her lip to hide her growing smile. She likes riling me up.

I hold out my hand. "Drink."

She scrunches her nose and makes an adorable purse of her lips like she's contemplating it. And then she goes to pour the contents into my hand.

I stop her before she tilts the liquid into my hand.

"Don't play with me—I'm not in the mood for games."

"That's too bad, because you already agreed to play our game tonight."

I huff as I pry the glass out of her fingers. "I need a dozen drinks first."

I down the liquid as I release her hand. When I glance back, she has two more full glasses in her hand. She quietly holds one out to me.

I set down my empty glass and take the new one, noticing the sparkle in her eyes. She likes playing games. And this time, she's out to win. She'll either learn more about me or get to commit another sin. And I have a feeling last night's sin was child's play compared to the plans in her head.

"I shouldn't have bought you."

"Oh? Why not?"

"Because you are going to be the death of me."

She smirks. "I'll drink to that."

We clink our glasses together. Our eyes never leave each other, even when we tilt our head back to drink the smooth whiskey.

The liquor isn't all I drink in—I greedily gobble up her body. She's wearing a pair of ripped jeans that hug her luscious hips. She found new heels, thank god. I almost regretted last night just because she lost her heels. A snug red top completes her look. She's let her hair down in long waves, but she's not wearing any makeup, not that she needs it. Her lashes are long, cheeks blush pink, and lips redder than any lipstick could match. She is beauty—makeup would only hide who she really is.

Her eyes take in my appearance as well. From my muddy boots to my overworked ripped jeans; my white T-shirt clinging to my body and covering enough of my tattoos that she can't tell what any of them are. She frowns when her eyes stop on top of my head.

I smirk—she doesn't like my man bun. I can see her imagination working, wishing my hair would fall down to my shoulders again. Most women hate my hair. They'd prefer me to chop it off. I don't know why I don't. Other than I've always worn my hair like this, and I'm too lazy to get a monthly haircut to keep up a shorter style.

She clears her throat as if to clear her mind. She's ridiculous for thinking about my body at all.

"Ready?" I ask.

She nods.

I follow her through the kitchen to the sitting room, the only room other than my bedroom she didn't completely destroy.

"What do I have to do to get you to spend some of your millions to hire someone to clean up this mess?" she asks before we reach the sitting room.

Her eyes meet mine again, and she blushes when she sees the heat in my eyes. She would have to willingly do some very dirty things for me to clean up her mess—things she will never voluntarily do.

Siren sits in the same armchair from last time we played this game. I notice the bottle of whiskey on the end-table and make a mental note to hide it after our game, if there is any left. I'm tired of her having the upper hand.

This time, instead of sitting on top of her or kneeling, I pull up one of the other chairs in the room and face it right across from her. This way, I won't miss a single expression she makes.

"Ladies first," I say.

She taps her fingers against her glass as she contemplates her single question. *Is she going to try to get answers from me, or is she going to try to get me to let her sin?*

She sighs, and I know I've already won before she even asks the question. Because tonight she is going to choose answers, even though she's burning to commit another sin. She thinks, in the long run, having more answers might mean losing this battle but eventually winning the war.

Unbeknownst to her, Siren has already won no matter what answers I give or sins she commits. She's already gotten me to silently vow to save her. In a few weeks, she will be free while my soul will belong to satan.

"Where are you from?"

I cock my head, trying to understand where she is going with this. *Why does it matter where I'm from? It doesn't. So what game is she playing? Does she think if she gets me to answer an easy question today that I'll answer a harder one tomorrow?*

"Are you sure that's the question you want to ask?" *More like a waste.*

She closes her eyes as if it pains her to ask. "Yes, my question is, where are you from?"

This is an easy question to dodge the truth on, while still giving her the truth. Before I came here, I lived in Miami. I spent most of my life there. At least I did when I wasn't out on one of Enzo's yachts.

But telling Siren I'm from Miami would be risking Enzo and my friend's lives. If Julian is listening, he would have probably heard of Enzo Black. He would know he's from Miami. He could piece together Enzo is my real boss. And I don't want Julian to know.

Siren doesn't realize the question she asked matters. She just wants to break through my walls and learn more about me. She wants to see if she can hitch a ride back to my home town. She can't—I would never take her to Miami.

I could tell her I'm from the ocean, but that would piss her off.

So I answer the only way I can. "New York." The place I was born. I lived there for less than nine months, but technically it answers her question. It's where I'm from.

Siren grins. "Zeke, from New York. I can work with that."

I frown, realizing now why she wanted to ask the question. All that is missing is my last name, and she would be able to search me in any database. She won't figure out my last name, but even if she did, New York knows nothing about who I really am.

She tucks her legs under her body, happy with her choice of question.

I shake my head. *How can she go from strong, gorgeous woman to sweet, innocent girl with one giddy smile and tuck of her legs?*

"Your turn," she says.

I could ask her the same question—use her strategy against her. I already know her first and last name. All I need is a location to find out everything. Although, if I wanted to research her right now, I could. I could find out everything with just her name.

But I'd rather find out everything from her. At least, until I'm forced to find out the truth. I'm nervous to face the truth, though, because honesty has a way of ruining everything. And I don't want whatever is flaring between us to disappear quite yet.

So I don't ask her where she is from. I consider my question for a moment, but I know the question I want answered.

"Who hurt you? Who made you hate men?"

Her eyes blink slowly, surprised by my question. She doesn't realize she wears her pain like a suit of armor. She oozes pride and defiance, a will to never let any man hurt her ever again. She is a woman who doesn't need a man.

Maybe it was getting kidnapped and then sold that made her hate men? Although, I think her hatred started long before Oscar found her. *Was Julian the one that hurt her? Or does her pain extend back a lifetime?*

Once she gets over her surprise at my question, her mind goes there—back to the day a man hurt her. Her body trembles slightly as she remembers. Her fear and pain ring through her body. Her eyes cloud over. She is no longer in this room—*she's there.* With *him*—I just don't know who *he* is.

I hate seeing her in pain and regret my decision immediately.

"Siren?"

Her head snaps to me, and her vision is gone.

"Who hurt you?" I ask again, with more caution in my voice. Now I must know. Because after I get Siren to safety, I'll hunt this predator down and kill him for ruining such a strong woman.

"Sin," she whispers. "I won't answer your question. I choose sin."

My shoulders fall; I won't be getting an answer out of her, at least not tonight.

I nod. "I reserve my sin until tomorrow." I stand to exit. With her memories of a vile man fresh in her mind, she isn't safe if I'm still here with her.

She hugs her knees to her chest. "Tomorrow is Friday."

"Yes, tomorrow is Friday."

"Julian?" she asks, her eyes pleading me to say I'm not bringing her, but I can't promise her that. I can't let Julian know I'm saving her until she's already safe.

"We are going. I'll decide tomorrow what my sin will be. Whether I sell you or claim you as my own. I expect you in bed within the hour, or you will have more than one punishment. Don't try to run; I won't be the only one who hunts you."

And then I leave, knowing within minutes, Siren will be in my bed next to me, hating me. Her hatred is for the best. Tomorrow I will commit a sin; it just isn't the sin Siren's expecting.

19

———

SIREN

I didn't sleep—not for a single second. I don't think Zeke slept either, although he never opened his eyes. His body tossed and turned in the bed as much as mine did. There was no snoring, no slow steady-rhythm breathing, no lifeless slumber.

We didn't sleep.

But we didn't talk either.

We didn't share our racing thoughts.

But Zeke didn't have to ask to know what I was thinking. He knows I'm terrified of Julian; he just doesn't know why. And he's not going to know why. Even if I end up going to Julian's tonight, Zeke is still going to be clueless as to the truth. But tonight could change everything for me—and it terrifies me.

As soon as dawn starts shining in through the bare windows, Zeke jumps out of bed. The room may be beautiful, but there is no way to sleep in, not when there aren't any curtains to keep the light out.

He doesn't speak to me as he walks down the hallway to the bathroom. I hear the flick of the water on.

And I carefully climb out of bed. When I hear the shower door open, I know now is my chance.

I need to run.

It's the only way I can stay safe.

If I start running, I will always be running.

Julian and Zeke will always be chasing me.

But I'd rather run the rest of my life than be ruined forever.

I tiptoe quickly through the house until I get to the back door. I don't want to run out the front. The front door leads to Julian; the beach and the ocean are to the back.

My plan is to swim out into the ocean and let the current carry me toward the pier where I can steal a boat and get off this island forever.

I open the door carefully, yet it screeches a little. The sliding door is rusty and in need of some WD40. But I can still hear the faint sound of the shower in the distance.

I take a deep breath, and then I run. Stripping my clothes down to my bra and underwear as I go. Down the steps. Across the beach. And into the water.

My safety.

My peaceful place.

My sanctuary.

The waves splash against my face as I sprint further into the water, and the feelings of security consume me. *My plan will work. I'll be safe, at least for tonight.* Tomorrow, I'll deal with the consequences of my decision. I just can't go to Julian's. I'd rather die than go back there.

Finally, I'm far enough out into the ocean that I can barely keep my head above the water as I wade. I dive under, feeling the connection to the water. I kick hard...once, twice, three times before I surface again and start breast-stroking down the beach. Each time I take a breath, I feel more alive than the previous. This is where I belong, chasing waves, not running from monsters.

Why didn't I do this the first night Zeke bought me?

Because as freeing as this feels, I'm also sealing my fate —I'm not really free. This is temporary. I have a lot of work left to do to make this permanent.

I dip back under the water, but this time I don't move with the wave. I'm jerked back by my ankle.

When I surface, I find myself pulled tightly against Zeke's shirtless body. I pant heavily, but I don't know if it's from the physical exertion or being so close to Zeke's body.

When I realize I'm not fighting, I push hard against him. He can't take me back. *He can't take me to Julian.*

But as soon as I break free, he grabs my wrist again, pulling me to him harder than ever. His force and our tension bruise my wrist.

"You're mine, Siren. I get to decide your fate, your future, your present."

"No," I pull hard, but his grip doesn't change. He's stronger than I will ever be. It doesn't stop me from fighting with everything that I have. "Let me go."

"No," he growls, pulling me up out of the water by my wrist until we are eye to eye.

He's pissed. Scared. Angry. I've never seen him so emotional before.

I stop fighting at his expression.

I'm not even sure I can breathe anymore without his permission.

"You. Are. Mine. You will follow my orders."

I nod, silently surrendering to him. My plan failed. I give in. And if Zeke didn't already have my fate planned out, he knows now. He can read on my face what will happen if he sells me to Julian.

"It's for your own good," he says so quietly that I'm not sure I even heard him.

I shake my head. Zeke has no idea what he is sentencing me to. He drags me through the water back to the beach. He doesn't stop. He doesn't breathe hard. He walks like he's walking on a treadmill, not dragging my ass through waves and sand.

When we reach the shore, Zeke throws me down harshly onto the sand. I fall, twisting, landing on my back, and my impact covers me in coarse sand. I'm only wearing my bra and panties, and I don't care what parts of me Zeke can see. This moment is the furthest thing from sexual.

Zeke stands over me, like the god he thinks he is. He may not have physically hurt me yet, but one way or another, I will be injured by the end of the night. Either Zeke will decide he wants me, in which case he will finally use me, or he'll sell me to Julian. And I'll get wounded worse than anything Zeke could ever imagine doing to me.

I close my eyes to keep the tears at bay. Running was a mistake. There is no way I was getting off this island, not when Julian owns every boat here. My only chance is Zeke. Him keeping me. He may only have a sliver of a heart, but at least he still has a piece of one. He may try to rape me, abuse me, torture me. But Zeke doesn't have Julian's experience. With Zeke, I have a chance at escaping. With Julian, I'll be dead by the end of the week.

"Don't sell me," I whisper.

Zeke doesn't answer. He doesn't flinch. He's not moved by my sobs.

Come—he commands with his body as he walks off. He doesn't even bother to speak to me.

My head falls as I push myself up off the sand. Running right now would only exhaust me. Zeke would catch me again, and bruise my other wrist. If Zeke is going to sell me to Julian, then I need all of my strength to fight my new enemy.

So I follow Zeke's command and accept my fate.

The rest of the day sludges by. We don't talk to each other. We eat in silence. And I spend most of the day in the shower, getting all my tears out and letting warmth sear my body. Once I'm inside Julian's house again, I'll be flooded with freezing fear.

I wear the most conservative, unflattering clothes I can find when I do finally get dressed. My baggiest jeans, tennis shoes, and an oversized sweatshirt. Even though it's warm outside, I need as many layers of protection as I can get. I wear my hair up in a high ponytail, using one of Zeke's scrunchies. At the last minute, I spot Zeke's razor next to the sink. I slip one of the blades out and into my back pocket. It's not much, but at least it's a weapon.

Strange how, in the last few days with Zeke, I haven't searched for a weapon. I haven't been afraid that Zeke was truly going to hurt me. This just proves how wrong I was. He may not be the one to lay a hand on me, but he's going to cause my suffering all the same.

Zeke's reflection pops into the mirror, just after I stash the razor. I stare at him blankly. If he realizes I have the blade in my pocket, he doesn't say anything.

We both stare, defying each other with our glances, but neither giving in. Any lust I felt for Zeke is long gone. I don't know why I was attracted to him for a single second. Physically he might be beautiful, but his heart is black. It doesn't matter how gorgeous he is on the outside, if he's a monster on the inside.

Zeke turns, and I follow automatically. We both walk slowly through the house. The sunset warms Zeke's appearance through the windows as we walk. He's wearing his usual jeans and a T-shirt, but this time he's added a leather jacket. I also see where he's carrying a gun in the back of his jeans.

He doesn't usually carry a gun; at least he doesn't around me. When I was going through his house, I didn't even find a gun locker or stash. Apparently, there are things in this house he's still hiding from me.

If Zeke's carrying a gun, it means he expects trouble tonight.

I'm not sure if that reassures me or terrifies me more. Julian is Zeke's business partner. He shouldn't expect any trouble going over for dinner to sell me to him. But he does. His steps aren't as purposeful as they usually are, almost like he might falter and change his mind.

We reach the front door.

Please, stay. We don't have to go. At least let me stay.

I feel his eyes cut back to me, but he doesn't turn his head full around to look at me. Maybe if he did, he'd choose differently. But he doesn't. He walks out to the truck, leaving me to follow.

Out of defiance, I leave the front door wide open as I exit. If Zeke notices, he doesn't care since he doesn't bother to go back and close it.

He just starts his truck and drives. Julian lives close enough that we could walk, but driving is probably better. I would purposefully walk at such a slow pace, it would take us all night to get there. Unfortunately, Zeke drives like he can't get to Julian's fast enough.

After parking the truck, Zeke gives me a look I can't read,

and then we both step out. Now that I'm here, I won't show fear. I'll walk in on my own will. And I'll fight with everything I have.

Zeke knocks once. It's loud enough to vibrate through the entire house.

I stand next to him proudly. I won't cower behind him like I did last time I saw Julian.

Of course, Julian isn't the one to open the door. That would be beneath him, so one of his men does. He nods at Zeke and holds the door for us to enter.

My eyes dart all around. My heart thumps on high alert the second my foot crosses the threshold. I'm ready for whatever Julian is going to do to me.

But I never get to the second step. I feel hands go all over my body as multiple men grab me. My mouth is gagged. My arms are pulled apart in either direction, and my ankles are tied together roughly, reminding me the tiny bruise Zeke caused when he grabbed my wrist was nothing. This is what real pain feels like, what real fear is like. I'd been spoiled living with Zeke these last few days.

The men start dragging my body away. I didn't even get to fight. I didn't have time to grab my weapon before I was ambushed.

Zeke doesn't even realize what happened until the last second, as I'm being dragged away.

His eyes connect with mine to witness my terror. Instantly, I force my pupils to change. *You did this. This is your fault. You knew better than to bring me here. Any pain I experience is on you. I hope you can sleep tonight knowing my pain is your fault.*

And just before I'm yanked out of his view, his eyes change too. Maybe it's my own stupid hope imagining the split-second change in his expression. Or maybe it's real. But I swore he promised me he wouldn't let anyone hurt me.

When I'm pulled into a dark room with half a dozen men, I realize it doesn't matter if the look in his eyes was real or not. Zeke won't be able to keep that promise.

20

───────

ZEKE

"Where is he?" I say, as I tear through the house looking for Julian.

One of his servants runs next to me, terrified. He tried to lead me to a sitting room, where he said Mr. Reed would join me in a minute.

I don't think so. I want to see the man—now.

I march up the stairs and find a locked door at the end of a hallway. A door I'm sure leads to his bedroom.

He better not be naked or fucking a woman right now, or I'll kill him. Nothing would stop me.

I kick the door down in one swift kick. He's not naked on the bed, thank god. I march through the room to the bathroom and find Julian spraying some aftershave on his face like nothing is happening—*fucking moron.*

"What the hell do you think you are doing?" I'm fuming. I thought I could hold back some of my anger, but I can't. I never agreed to Julian tying up Siren and dragging her to god knows where as soon as I entered his house. I agreed to bring her. I agreed to show her off in front of potential clients—nothing more.

Apparently, my rage isn't afraid of ruining everything by throwing a punch at this man. I do it anyway.

The crack of his jaw is music to my ears.

But one punch isn't enough. I grab his shoulders and shove him into the closet door behind him. His head bounces off the door as his eyes see stars.

I snarl. The man may be the leader of a criminal organization, but he can't fight for shit. He hasn't defended himself. He hasn't tried to throw a punch. He hasn't even reached for a gun.

He starts sliding to the floor, but I grab his shirt collar and hold him eye to eye with me. His feet dangle on the floor.

"What. Did. You. Do?" I growl. I'm not letting him go until I get some answers. And depending on his answers, I still might not free him.

He spits blood out to the right as he cracks his neck and takes his time answering me. I'll give him credit—he's not cowering in front of me like I'd expect an inexperienced man to.

"Put me down, and I'll tell you," Julian says, adjusting his jaw side to side.

I place him on his feet, but don't let go of the collar of his pristine white shirt. Somehow I managed not to get a drop of blood on it. I'll change that quickly if he doesn't start talking.

"I needed to make sure your pet was secure while we had dinner," Julian says.

I shake my head. "She's obedient to me. You didn't need to tie her up in order for her to behave herself."

"But then you might be distracted, and I need you on your game in order to convince these men to place a big shipment. Getting the deal with Oscar means nothing if we can't sell the women for a high price."

"You had no right to touch her. She's mine. I'm the one who has been slowly breaking her in. I'm the one who paid millions of dollars to enjoy her, not you."

"And I'm the one who cuts your paychecks so you could afford to buy her in the first place."

I raise my eyebrows. "You paid me thirty million dollars? Hmm…because my bank account says you've paid me far less. I guess I earned that money long before I ran into you."

"You wouldn't be alive without me. You owe me."

I don't argue. "Where is she?"

"She's safe—locked up in a room in the basement with a dozen guards watching over her. They are under strict instructions to only tie her up and protect her with their lives. I know how much she's worth to you. I won't let any harm come to her. But my offer still stands, I'll buy her from you. Name your price. From your reaction, I can tell the sex alone must be worth every penny."

I growl again.

He smirks.

I'm still gripping his shirt.

But his eyes hold no fear. He's in control. He's the boss, not me. I've never been the boss, even when I worked for a good man, my life still wasn't my own.

I could probably ask for sixty million, and Julian would pay it. He has the money. And he wants to take something from me, even if he pays for it.

But I'd never sell Siren. Even though she thinks differently—Julian will never touch her.

"Siren isn't for sale. She's mine," my voice is throaty and low, deeper than a crack of thunder.

"We'll see. I'm guessing you'll be begging me to buy her soon."

Julian's eyes glance down at where I'm still gripping him. "Now our guests will be arriving shortly. It's time to go make some money."

I release him, hating this. I want Siren with me, not locked up somewhere. When I get her home, I'm going to pay for her being locked up. I'll have to sleep with one eye open because Siren will certainly try something. This is definitely worthy of her cutting off my dick.

Julian wipes the blood from his mouth. The bruising won't set in until tomorrow, so his guests will never know I hit him. Then he grabs his suit jacket and puts it on before I follow him downstairs to the dining room. His other guests have already arrived.

"Welcome, everyone. Sorry for the delay," Julian says, walking up to the first man.

"So glad you could make it, Mr. Palmer," Julian says.

"I would never miss a dinner of yours, Mr. Reed," he answers.

"This is my right-hand man, Zeke," Julian says.

I shake the man's hand sternly, even though I'd rather rip it off. I can see his dark heart without knowing anything about him.

Julian introduces me to a short, balding man and his wife next—a Mr. and Mrs. Gibson. Bile rises in my throat, realizing a woman is involved in buying other women. Somehow it seems worse that she would betray her own sex.

The last man I'm introduced to is younger, closer to my age. He, like me, doesn't like to be called by his last name. Instead, he goes by Rafael.

Julian motions for us all to take a seat. Julian sits on the end of the table, and I'm seated on his right with everyone else filed around.

Servants stream in, pouring everyone a drink, and bringing out appetizers. I force myself to eat calamari even though I'm not the least bit hungry.

"So tell us, when will the next shipment be in?" Mr. Palmer asks.

Julian shovels food into his mouth. Apparently, he wants me to answer the mundane questions.

"Two weeks," I say.

Mr. Palmer sounds surprised, "So long?"

"Yes, we want to ensure we get the highest quality for you to choose from."

"Hmm," his wife, Mrs. Gibson, murmurs, not believing me.

"We also hand-deliver your selection to ensure your order gets there swiftly and without any complications," I say, like I'm talking about a shipment of drugs instead of women.

Everyone nods.

"Tell me, what type of women and how many each of you might be interested in? We'd like to make the best selections for you," Julian says.

We go around the room listening to each of Julian's guests describe in vivid detail the kind and quantity of women they want to buy. It's clear we won't be able to get rid of any more than twenty to this group of buyers, but they have connections who would be happy to take more if the quality is high, according to Mr. Gibson. And these four would pay fifty million dollars a piece for a high-quality woman.

"Again, you still haven't convinced us of the quality of

your women." Mr. Palmer says, shoving half a lobster into his mouth after drowning it in butter.

Julian smiles. He snaps his fingers.

My next sight hits me down to my bones.

Siren is dragged into the room, tied up with ropes and three men guarding her. Her mouth is gagged, and she fights hard against the ropes.

Julian nods to one of the guards, and he rips the sweater from her body. The look in her eyes is one meant to kill.

She fights harder, and I have no doubt if she fought for long enough, she'd find a way to free herself. You can see it in all her body language. And everyone in the room witnesses it too. I quickly look around and see how much every person in the room wants her—*my woman.*

My blood boils red. I can't make a scene here. It would ruin everything. I need Julian to think I'm as bad as him, so when I leave this damn island, he will have no reason to follow. I'll have paid my debt.

But after this, after what he did to Siren, I can't just bounce. Julian will pay for this.

21

SIREN

I'M NOT a woman who asks for help often. But today—I'm asking for help. Because I already know how this ends.

I have rope burn all over my body. My agitated skin will have marks and welts for at least a week where the rope digs into my skin. At least the physical marks won't be permanent. But the emotional scars, they will stay with me forever.

This isn't my first time in Julian's house. I know what he has planned next. And being tied up, dragged out in front of a group of people enjoying dinner, while embarrassing, is nothing compared to what comes next.

I try to get free, but I'm not strong enough to take on three grown men, much less the ropes binding my arms and legs. I shake my head, trying to get the gag to loosen from my mouth. I manage enough for my cries to start sounding less like moans and more like real words. But I can't get the gag off, and my cries for help sound like I'm enjoying myself, not afraid for my life. So eventually, I force myself to remain silent. These people don't deserve to hear me.

My eyes defy every person in the room. The single old

man. The gross couple. The young man. Julian snickering at the head of the table. And finally—Zeke.

I shouldn't have looked at Zeke. I know it immediately when our eyes lock. He can't help me, and that devastates me. Because he's the only one who can...

Once I look at him, I can't look away. I plead for him to help with my eyes. And his eyes respond with *I can't.*

Everything else in his body screams a different promise. *I'll burn this fucking island down for you.*

His face is red, his nostrils flare like a bucking bull, and his jaw ticks with the full force of his anger. The veins in his neck bulge as blood circulates faster, flooded with adrenaline. He's suffering under the stress of a decision—saving me and ruining his relationship with Julian, or doing nothing to save face.

I don't know which he's going to choose. If logic wins out, I'm toast. But I can tell his heart thinks differently. His heart wants to save me.

I almost wish he wouldn't save me. I'll ruin his soul, and he won't deserve the pain.

Zeke's body has hardened, and I can't tell if his muscles are pumping up ready for a fight, or his brain won and his body is just tense as he forces it to stay in his chair.

Unfortunately, Julian decides not to stay in his chair. He stands and takes his time walking over to me.

"All the women we bring you will be of similar quality as this one. Expensive breeding, exquisite body, and a fight you will enjoy taming."

I scream as I pull against the ropes as Julian approaches.

The woman laughs. "She's wonderful. Is she for sale?"

Julian looks at Zeke, who looks like he's going to murder everyone in the room.

"Sorry, I don't believe she's for sale," Julian finally

answers. "But worry not, we will only bring you women of the same caliber."

There are murmurs throughout the room.

"Come, see for yourself what a treat she is," Julian says, waving the group over.

No.

I won't let them touch me.

I have too much self-respect.

I have control over who touches me and who doesn't.

Zeke sits up straighter, seconds away from launching himself across the table. I want him to save me, but not from this. *This, I got.*

So I give Zeke a wink. He blinks rapidly, not sure he saw me do it. It makes me smile slightly. He cocks his head, confusion on his face.

This time, I save myself, but you owe me, Zeke. Soon, I won't be able to.

He nods at me, and then I focus on my target—the woman. She disgusts me more than anyone else here. And if I take her out, this charade will stop. They will focus on helping her, not on parading me around the room for their pleasure. They will hate me.

The old man approaches and grabs my chin—I let him. He inspects my face like a racehorse he's about to buy.

The next man grabs my waist, pulling me toward him until I smell his whiskey breath and plump belly against my stomach. At least his stomach protrudes enough to shield me from feeling any erection he might have under all that blubber.

The young man keeps his distance, observing from afar. He pretends to be uninterested, although I know differently. It doesn't make him any more moral than anyone else here.

Finally, the woman approaches. She takes her time

looking me over with a bright smile, and then, she goes for my breast. *Not today, lady.*

The guards are holding my arms tightly out on either of my sides, with the third guard standing behind me. My feet are tied together at my ankles. I can't break free of the ropes, so I use them.

As the men hold me up, I throw my weight back onto my arms, lift my legs, and kick her hard in the chest with both my feet.

The woman falls back, like she's just been shot.

I laugh beneath my gag as the guards stand in shock, not sure what to do. The potential buyers bend down to help the woman. She struggles to breathe, and she'll have a nasty bruise over her heart for a few days. I'm sure I'll get punished for the move by the guards or Julian, but it will be worth it.

Julian walks over, observing my victim calmly, and without any intention of helping. Instead, he turns and looks at me with fury in his eyes.

Serves you right for treating me worse than an animal.

"Get her out of here," Julian says to the guards.

I'm starting to get dragged out, when Zeke stands up.

Yes! Now is the time to save me. Because if I leave this room without you, the scars they'll inflict will never leave me.

Julian steps in front of me, facing Zeke. I can see the side of Julian's expression. He's telling Zeke to fix this. Close the deal, or else.

Or else what? What does Julian have over Zeke?

When my view of Zeke is unblocked, I look at him, but he's no longer looking at me, he's looking at the mess on the floor and how he's going to salvage it.

No...

Zeke...

Julian returns his gaze to me, and I see the devil in his eyes. I know what comes next.

The guards pull me out of the room, away from Zeke.

Zeke doesn't follow.

He stays. He sentences me to my fate.

If he lets me leave with Julian, he won't be able to save me.

The guards drag me up the stairs and into Julian's bedroom. I'm tossed to the floor. My body slams against the wood floor. The guards leave as Julian enters the room.

The familiar sound of the lock on the door closing behind him skyrockets my anxiety.

Julian takes his time walking over; he's like Zeke in that way. *How could two men be so similar and yet treat me so differently?*

Julian yanks me to my feet, and I'm left standing in the middle of the room, still tied around my arms and legs. My mouth is still gagged. I have the ability to fight—to at least delay Julian's fury and give Zeke more time to rescue me.

But I'm frozen. I can't move. I can't react. Julian is the only man in the world I can't fight back against.

It wouldn't make sense to most people. But it's my reality. That's why Julian scares me more than most men. Every other man I can fight against. He may still win, but at least I have a chance. With Julian, I'm helpless.

Julian undoes the button holding his jacket together. He slips it off carefully and hangs it over the back of a chair in the corner. Then he slowly rolls up his sleeves. Each of his movements taunt me. My imagination is worse than what will really happen—or at least that's what I keep telling myself.

Julian grins at me as he takes a step closer, and I don't back up. He's won already. He controls me.

"Such a pretty girl, but you didn't dress very pretty for me tonight, pet."

I close my eyes. I need to disappear, at least in my head. It's the only way to survive.

But Julian won't allow that. *What fun would he have in hurting me if he couldn't see the pain all over my face?*

He grabs my chin and uses his other hand to pry my left eye open. It burns being forced open.

And then he spits.

I close my eye quickly, but some of his saliva still enters my eye—*disgusting.* I try opening, but it stings. I blink, trying to see again, but I can't. *What was in his saliva? Pepper? Alcohol? It's fucking alcohol.* I smell the whiskey.

"Look at me, pet."

I can't, I try to say, but it comes out as a moan.

I look at him with my good eye, and his lips curl up higher, loving my sounds.

I won't make any more. That was the last you will get from me, you bastard.

I swallow down the pain. It's just my eye. I'm sure with some water, it will be better. My eye is the least of my worries.

I have to frequently close and re-open my eyes so I don't seem like I'm crying. It's when I have my eyes closed that he chooses to attack.

His hit is a semi-truck right to my jaw. It takes my breath away and gives me a splitting headache. I'm sure I heard bones break. It will take me weeks to be able to eat properly.

I fall to my knees from the explosion of pain in my head. I try to open my eyes, to prepare for the next attack.

"You can thank your boyfriend for that. He punched me in the jaw; it's only polite to return the favor."

Zeke punched Julian? Somehow that makes me feel a little

better. I'm not sure what Zeke and Julian's relationship is exactly. Zeke doesn't call him Mr. Reed like everyone else, and Julian doesn't seem to care. Yet, Zeke still works for him, makes money for him. I don't understand.

"And this, this is because I like breaking pretty things."

No!

It's too late. My breath is gone as he kicks me in the chest. My ribs crack, and I'm afraid my heart stopped at the jolt.

I fall over to my side. *I'm helpless. Powerless. I can't win.* And Zeke will be too late. I already know.

I look to the door through my burning tears. The tears from my left eye spill to the right. I close my eye tightly, but some of the drops get in, burning my right eye as well.

I close them both tightly, refusing to open again. I have no hope that Zeke will come, at least not until it's all over. For all I know, he's already sold me to Julian. That's why he let him take me. And he's downstairs getting the other men to agree to a payment of their own.

Zeke will leave here rich, while I'll leave here broken and in someone else's charge.

I feel more hits, but they barely register. He's already broken me; everything else is just scattering the pieces. The first hit is always the worst; this is nothing.

Until everything changes. Getting hit is one thing, but getting raped...

I feel him rip my clothes with a blade pushed against my skin, leaving my bindings intact, until I'm wearing only my underwear.

I beg through my eyes, giving him one final plea, hoping he has some level of consciousness beneath his rough exterior.

Please.

I hold my gaze on his as a single tear falls down my face. Then another, and another.

"God, I love it when you beg."

With one final rip, I'm naked except for the ropes. I have no clothes left to protect me. Julian is done beating me.

I was wrong when I said the first blow is the worst. If I was only getting beaten, that statement would be true. But what comes next will obliterate me. There will be nothing left of me to put back together.

Siren will be gone. And I don't know who will replace me.

22

ZEKE

I DON'T LIKE that I can no longer see Siren. But being locked away somewhere is safer than being in this room, with these horrible people. As soon as I finish closing this deal, I'll get her and leave.

I still have a sin to use against her from our game yesterday, but I've already sinned enough. I'll answer any question she has and let her commit any sin against me.

Because I failed her.

I didn't protect her.

She's spent her night tied up in ropes because of me.

I walk over to the huddle of men and the injured woman Siren kicked in the chest. *Serves her right.* I wish I could do the same to all of them without pissing off Julian.

"Need any help? Should I call for the doctor?" I ask.

"No, no, that won't be necessary," the woman's husband says. He strokes her face. "Feeling better, dear?"

Dear? God, they disgust me. He's calling his wife by an endearment when they came here to buy another woman for him to stick his nasty dick into.

She nods, and the men help her sit up. She grasps her chest, her breathing hard and painful.

Good.

"She just knocked the wind out of me. That was some woman," she says.

At least she got something right; Siren is definitely some woman—she's my woman.

"Maybe we should continue these discussions next week? You should probably get some rest; you took quite a hit," I say, just wanting this night over. I'll wine and dine them again; I just want to get Siren out of here as fast as possible.

"No, no. That won't do. We have a flight scheduled for tomorrow afternoon," the husband says.

"Well, would you like to discuss some numbers then?" I ask. *Please say no. Say you don't want to do business with us after Siren hurt your wife.*

"Yes, let's do."

Ugh.

I spot a stack of documents in the corner of the dining room Julian seems to have had drawn up for this meeting. *Where is Julian anyway?*

I spot one of the servants. "Do you know where Jul—I mean, Mr. Reed disappeared to?"

He nods and whispers. "He had some blood on his shirt. He's just changing but said to have you finish up here."

I sigh.

I pick up the documents and look them over quickly, knowing the faster I get this finished, the faster I get to see Siren. I'm not waiting on Julian to get back.

The contracts discuss the payment and delivery timeline the client would like for "goods." No mention of selling women. Smart not to put something so incriminating down on paper.

I sit down in Julian's seat, not because I want to sit there, but because it gives me the best view of everyone.

"So how many would you like delivered to you? We can offer a slight deal on larger orders. But if you want the absolute best we find, those come at a premium price." *Fuck me.* I deserve everything coming my way for this meeting alone.

The wife and husband exchange glances, and then she looks at me giddily. "We want the woman who was here before."

I cock an eyebrow. "The woman who kicked you?"

I don't understand why they would want Siren when she nearly killed this woman. If she wasn't tied up, I have no doubt she would have succeeded.

"Yes, we want her. I love a woman with that much spirit. A woman like her takes so much longer to break. We will pay a premium price for her," the wife says.

"She isn't for sale," I answer.

The wife looks to her husband, who takes over. "I'm sure we can come to a financial agreement."

"She's not for sale." *No woman should be.*

"Twenty million."

"She's not for sale," my voice is annoyed and deep. *He's pushing me too far.*

"Thirty million."

"She's not for sale."

"Fifty million."

"She's not for sale."

"One hundred million."

The room falls silent—all eyes go to me. Julian would kill me for not taking the deal. He just offered a hundred million for Siren, more than triple what I paid for her.

It's an insane amount of money.

But once again, I have to state the obvious.

I stand, putting my fists down on the table, rattling the tableware. "She. Is. Not. For. Sale. She's mine." My voice shakes the entire room, like an earthquake just hit the house.

Everyone is silent. No one says anything while I stare them down.

This is not a negotiation.

This is not something I will back down on.

If it's the last thing I do, I'll make sure Siren gets off this island and safely away from these people.

Rafael breaks the silence. "I'll take five at ten million a piece. Plus, I have some close friends who will each want at least five as well."

I write down the deal. I don't care about negotiating for more money at this point. I just want this over.

I slide the contract and pen over to him.

He reads it over carefully and signs it before sliding it back to me.

I nod at him.

"It was pleasure doing business with you, Zeke. Tell Mr. Reed I retired to my room for the night and look forward to doing more business with you in the future."

I nod again but don't shake his hand. I can't stand to touch any one of them right now.

He picks up his drink and then whistles casually as he walks out.

"I want three," the older man says.

Again, I fill out the paperwork, then he signs and leaves.

I turn to the remaining couple. "And what can I do for you?"

"We want your best ten. If they are as good of quality as you claim, we will pay up to fifty million a piece."

I nod, agreeing.

I fill in the blanks on the contract and then slide it over to the couple to read.

The couple takes fucking forever to read every word of the contract. It's probably a smart move considering who Julian is, but my anxiety is rising with every passing minute.

I expected Julian to have returned by now, but he hasn't. *Maybe he's letting me finish the contracts by myself? He thinks we will get a better deal if I do the negotiations? Or he wants me to show how skilled I am?*

But it makes me feel uneasy. I don't know where Siren is. Julian knows he can't touch her. I would kill him for a look in her direction, let alone a touch. He promised he would unleash her as soon as the meeting was over. So hopefully she's just locked up in a room somewhere.

But if I know my girl, she's pissed. She should be making a lot of racket, slamming on doors and stomping her feet to show me how disappointed she is in me. But I hear nothing.

Either Julian's house is more soundproof than most, or Siren is still tied up.

I glance over at the couple, imploring them to fucking sign the papers already.

Finally, they sign.

I stand and rip the papers from them, preparing to exit the room. "Excuse me," I say. It's the last words I ever want to say to any of them. Because if I meet them again, I'll kill them all for thinking women are items for sale.

When I exit the dining room, I crane my neck, trying to listen to any sign of Siren. But I hear nothing.

Where are you, baby? I know you hate me right now, but you need to tell me where you are.

There is a door that leads down to the basement, and a grand staircase that leads upstairs. *Which should I choose?*

I see a servant standing, watching me from the hallway.

He doesn't speak, but his eyes tilt up.

She's upstairs.

I run up the stairs, three at a time.

My breathing picks up as I look left then right. There is a long hallway to each side. With closed door after door.

I hear a noise from my right. The tiniest of cries— Siren's.

No.

No. No. No.

Please no.

I can't have failed her this badly. *Please, don't let her be hurt. I won't survive seeing her in pain. That's my greatest weakness. Fuck, no.*

I run down the hallway and twist the door handle. It's locked.

I step back and kick with everything I have. The door splits, but it's thicker than most. A door built to keep sound and people in.

Fuck. Why did I bring Siren tonight? I could have closed that deal without her. I should have stood up to Julian.

I kick again, and the door splits enough for me to push through the splintered wood.

The sight I see destroys me.

Siren is naked on the floor. Ropes still bind her arms and legs. Her mouth is still gagged. But otherwise, everything that made Siren herself has been beaten out. So much blood covers her skin. Bruises are already coloring her broken layers. Her legs are spread, and Julian is settled between them.

I don't know if he's entered her yet.

But I already know I failed. No apology will ever be enough to make this up to her. She will never forgive me for letting this happen—*never*.

And I'll never be able to forgive myself.

But what guts me the most is her tears. *Her beautiful, fucking tears.* She's been completely ruined. She doesn't cry unless she's really hurting. I could snap her arm, break every bone, and she wouldn't cry. She's too proud. She wouldn't want to give Julian the pleasure of seeing her in pain.

Yet, here she is showing him every drop of pain—showing me. And it's all my fault.

I explode—headfirst at Julian.

I pound him into the floor with all my might, getting him as far away from Siren as I can.

And then I start punching, over and over and over. "I'm going to kill you! You hear that? You're a dead man!"

More punches. More kicks.

I forget about everything except killing this man. I'm a trained killer. One snap of his neck. One jab to the throat. One shot of my gun. One slice to the heart. There are so many different ways I could kill him—so many choices.

But I don't want to kill him quickly; I want him to die slowly and tortuously for what he did. For the mess he caused. And how much I'm going to have to clean up after he's dead. How many more men are going to have to die because of him.

I'm going to spend the rest of my life running and fighting, away from my family of friends, until I've killed every man loyal to this bastard. Instead of being free of him in a matter of weeks.

It will be worth it though to avenge Siren.

Moans...*Siren! I completely forgot about her.*

I punch Julian hard one more time in the face, knocking him completely out. I need to tend to Siren; then I can decide his fate.

I run over to Siren and find her stirring, groaning in pain. She shivers from the cold, and if I'm not careful, she'll lose too much blood to recover.

Siren has to be my focus right now as much as I want to kill Julian. I consider pulling my gun out and shooting him dead. But that wouldn't be enough to satisfy me or Siren. She's going to want him tortured. I'll come back for him later.

Right now, I need to protect Siren.

I pull my shirt off and wrap it around her body as best I can. I loosen the gag, and it falls around her neck.

"You're going to be okay; I've got you," I whisper into her hair, not caring if Julian hears me or not. She's mine, not his. If I choose to be kind to her, that's my prerogative.

"This is going to hurt, just for a minute. But I'm going to make you feel better soon. I promise."

She sighs, her eyes still shut with tears falling quickly. I lean down to kiss her cheek but stop short. I don't get to kiss her when I'm the reason she's in pain.

The stench of alcohol hits my nose—her tears. The bastard poured alcohol into her eyes; no wonder she's crying.

Carefully, I place my arms under her neck and legs. I force my eyes to avoid looking between her legs. I don't want to know if he raped her or not. Because if he did, I wouldn't be able to leave without killing him first.

Once Siren is settled in my arms, I stand and face Julian, who is starting to stir.

"This isn't over," I say.

He coughs up blood. "You're right; it's not."

I kick him one more time for good measure, and then I leave. I race down the stairs, trying my best not to jostle Siren too much, but I know she needs out of this house as fast as possible.

My truck is parked out front, and I'm grateful I drove the truck instead of walking. But I don't want her out of my arms, even for the two-minute drive to my house.

So I push the driver's chair all the way back and hold her in my lap as I drive home.

"Please, be okay. Please, forgive me. Please…"

23

SIREN

I CAN'T OPEN my eyes, but I'm still aware of everything happening.

I hear Zeke kick Julian's ass.

I feel him carry me in his arms. I should hate him. He's the reason I'm hurting. But in his strong arms, I feel safe, protected.

Stupid mind thinking I could ever be secure with a man.

I feel him holding me tighter to his chest on his lap, like a wounded bird. *That's what I am? Wounded? Broken? A goddamn disaster.*

I feel every bump in the truck as he drives us back, but I try my best not to whimper. I want to be back at Zeke's house as soon as possible, even if I have to deal with a little extra pain.

And then I feel Zeke carry me into the house. He flicks lights on as he goes. I moan as the brightness stings my eyes even though they are still closed.

"I'm sorry, but I need to be able to see your wounds to help you," Zeke whispers, like each word pains him.

Even though the gag is gone, I still don't speak in

anything but moans and groans. Julian took my voice, along with everything else.

I hear Zeke sweep something onto the floor, and then he lays me down on the dining room table.

I shiver as the cool hits my back.

"Hold on," Zeke says.

I chuckle on the inside. *There is nothing for me to hold onto, you idiot.*

Time does weird things when you are in pain. A second later, or maybe an hour, Zeke returns. He places a thick blanket over me.

"I'm going to check over your wounds, okay? I need to stop any bleeding and make sure nothing needs stitches."

He waits. He's asking me for fucking permission to heal me. *It's too fucking late to ask for permission now, you prick!* You should have asked me before you bought me. Before you tried to sell me.

He waits a second longer, then curses under his breath. He must have decided he's out of time to get permission.

He checks over my head first, placing a bandage on my forehead. I hear him hiss when he gets to my jaw. But he doesn't say anything.

He examines my neck next. He must decide it's okay, because he quickly moves to my chest and stomach.

He gasps—*it must be bad.*

I feel something stick into my arm. He's giving me drugs. The warmth spreads quickly, and I instantly feel light as a feather. I'm floating above all the pain. It's still there, the pain, but it doesn't control me anymore.

I try to see what he's doing, but it's still too painful to open my eyes.

I feel his hands work on my stomach. He's probably

stitching me up, but he must be very skilled at it because I don't feel the stick of a needle or the pull of thread.

I feel him cut the rope from my arms, remove the gag dangling from my neck, and re-wrap the blanket around my torso. Then he frees my legs as well.

The blanket is covering most of my body, but I feel him hesitate before lifting it up to see between my legs.

Almost instantly, he lowers the blanket again. Either I look normal, or there is too much damage for him to fix.

And then I feel his hand against my face, stroking me gently.

"I need to wash out your eyes," he says.

He's right, but I don't want to open my eyes. I'm not sure how he knows my eyes need washing out.

"I'm going to get some water, and then I'm going to stop the burning."

He doesn't ask me for permission this time, knowing I won't answer him right now. I hear the faucet run, and then he's by my side again.

He takes my hand and places it on his forearm.

"Squeeze hard," he commands. I do as he says. Gently opening my left eye, he begins flushing out the alcohol.

I squeeze his forearm as he pushes more water through my eye. Eventually, I feel the sting soften. He lets go of my eye, and I close it gently to prepare for him to flush the other one.

He doesn't give me time to think about the pending pain. He just moves to the next eye and does what needs to be done. I squeeze hard as pain stings my eye, but it too dissipates.

Zeke stops.

And I keep my eyes closed.

My breathing steadies.

The discomfort eases.

And Zeke—he's still here.

Time passes as my exhausted body falls into a restless sleep from the drugs Zeke pushed through me. At first, I fight it. I don't trust Zeke, or any man, when I'm under the pull of drugs. But I need rest to heal.

"You're safe," he whispers. "I won't let anyone hurt you. Ever again. Including me."

And with those unreal promises ringing in my ears, I drift to sleep.

———

I WAKE IN A SOFT BED. I'm lying in the middle with pillows all around me. I'm in Zeke's bed, so I expect to see him sleeping next to me.

But when I open my eyes, I find him kneeling next to the bed, his head bent, his hands clasped together and folded. I recognize the position—my father was a religious man. He'd pray every night before getting into bed.

Zeke can't be praying, though? Is he?

"Are you praying?" I ask, looking at him suspiciously.

His head pops up suddenly. All kinds of emotions cross his face—joy, fear, pain. His face finally settles on a reserved expression hiding his emotions.

"I'm not religious. And if God exists, I would be one of the last people he would listen to. But I had to try. Your heartbeat was so weak. I couldn't understand why. You didn't lose much blood, from what I could see. I assumed you were bleeding internally. And if you were, I wouldn't be able to get you to a decent hospital in time. All I could do was pray."

My mouth drops.

"What did you pray?"

"I begged for you to stay."

I gulp. He looks so sincere—in so much pain, watching me.

I don't know how long I've been out, but it doesn't look like he's slept. Julian's blood still speckles with mine all over Zeke's clothes. His hair is barely held up by his scrunchie. His eyes are bloodshot. And he looks to be in physical pain.

"Are you injured?" I ask.

"Not physically," he answers. *Just emotionally.*

I blink, not understanding how he's hurting emotionally.

"You didn't sell me?" I meant my words to be a statement, but they come out as a question. *Did he sell me? Was he just pissed at Julian for touching me before the money had been transferred?*

He's silent a moment, still as a statue. But his eyes pour into mine, giving me everything. Then he says, "I lied. I never planned on selling you and I never will."

What? My eyebrows reach epic levels on my forehead. *He lied?*

"I know it means you get to kill me now, but can you at least wait until I apologize first?" he smiles gently, testing the waters with me.

It's a damn gorgeous smile—complete with a shy dimple I didn't notice before, but all I can focus on is what he just said. *He wants to apologize?!* I don't think anyone, especially a man, has apologized to me before.

"Can you reserve your punishment until I finish speaking?" he asks.

"You didn't lie during our game."

He nods.

"Then I don't get to punish you. The rules only apply to

the game."

He nods again, with a brighter smile, but then he exhales harshly. "I'm sorry."

Two words.

Words that change my life.

My heart starts hammering faster.

My breath is deeper.

Colors are more vivid in the room.

And Zeke's smell fills my nostrils fully for the first time.

I come alive with those words.

Zeke studies my expression as he speaks.

I close my eyes to keep new tears at bay. "Again," I whisper.

"I'm sorry," he says.

"Again."

"I'm sorry, Siren. I'm so sorry," his voice cracks in pain. It's the most beautiful sound. *So fucking beautiful.* I've never heard anything so beautiful.

He clears his throat and tries again. "I'm sorry I lied to you about selling you. I'm sorry I brought you to Julian's. I'm sorry I let the guards tie you up. I'm sorry I let them take you away. I'm sorry I let Julian hurt you. I'm sorry..." and then he's not speaking anymore.

I open my eyes and watch him break. Tears are falling.

Down.

Down.

Down.

Tiny droplets coat his cheeks and drop to his shoulders.

I've never seen a grown man cry. Up until this point, I didn't think men ever cried, at least not in front of other people.

But here he is crying for me. For my pain. For what he did to me.

I don't understand this man.

I don't understand why he bought me.

I don't understand why he didn't protect me.

But the most surprising thing...I don't know when I started falling for him.

It's the stupidest thing I could have done—*fall*.

Zeke may care for me, but he's also going to get me killed one day. I shouldn't want anything to do with him, yet I do. I want to experience everything with him.

He was the first man to save me.

The first man to say he's sorry.

The first man to promise to protect me.

And that means everything.

I might risk my heart again, even if I already know the outcome. Maybe for a little bit, I can live in this moment of pure happiness. It may not be love, but it could be fucking close.

"What happened?" I ask, needing to know everything.

"Julian played me. He wanted you, and I was stupid enough to think he was on my side. I'm sorry."

I nod. That's who Julian is. He has this ability to hide his monster until he's ready to show it to you, and by then it's too late.

"I'm going to kill him for touching you."

More tears spring to my eyes. I want that so badly, but it can't happen for so many reasons Zeke has yet to realize.

"No, I don't want you to."

He frowns.

"Just keep me safe from him. Promise?"

"I promise."

And I'll hold him to that vow.

"What happened?" Now it's Zeke's turn to ask.

"Julian...hurt me."

Zeke wants to know more. *Did he rape me? Did he push inside me?* That's what he's really asking.

"Was I too late?" Zeke asks.

I pause. That's such a complicated question to answer. I try to think, but most of what happened is a blur. My brain pushed it out. Whether Julian raped me or not doesn't matter. Because what he is really asking is—is it too late for us? Too late to change our future? Too late for us to choose love over hate?

And that answer is going to hurt.

Him.

Me.

"Yes, you were too late," I answer honestly with burning tears.

Zeke's eyes scorch too.

I wipe my eyes, needing to change the subject.

"How about that sin you still have to commit? What will it be?" I ask, needing him to do anything, make me feel anything but this heartache.

Zeke could have been the one. The one to be strong enough.

Man enough.

Loving enough.

But now it's too late—and I may have just missed my one chance at ever knowing love.

Zeke smiles sadly. "I've sinned enough for one night."

I sigh. I agree. But we need something to get rid of the tension—something to push our thoughts away from what happened.

"How about a new game of truth or sin?" I ask.

He nods—of course, he does. Right now, I don't think Zeke would deny me anything. And somehow that terrifies me.

24

ZEKE

I was too late.

I was too fucking late.

Those two words, *too late*, will end me.

I thought we might be at a beginning after I saved her, not an end. I finally finished debugging the house. I can tell her the truth. I'm ready to face Julian Reed head-on. I could get her out of here.

But now, I don't know.

She hates me, with good reason. If I told her the truth right now, she wouldn't even believe me.

And now she wants to play a game of truth or sin.

Like I have the energy for that.

But I'll deny her nothing right now. I'd bring her Julian's head on a platter if she demanded it. I'd jump into a fire just so she could watch me burn. I'd do anything, fucking anything, for her.

And she knows it.

So if she wants me to play, I'll play. But I don't want to hurt her. I can't sin against her. That is the one request I can't fulfill.

"I'll play under one condition," I say.

She frowns. "What?"

"If you don't answer the question, you get to choose your sin against me, not me." My voice is vulnerable. I'm telling her exactly who I am in this moment—weak, weak for her.

She's wanted control this entire time. Well, now she has it, all of it. I'm giving it all to her—every single drop. I have nothing left. I won't order her with my voice or my unspoken commands. I'll ask nothing of her, ever again.

She nods and gathers herself.

I've long given up stopping the heavy flow of tears. I rarely cry. But I am a sensitive person, so it does happen, just usually not in front of someone else. I can normally wait until I'm by myself to let loose.

"You go first," I say.

Lines form around her eyes and mouth as she thinks. It's adorable as always and distracts me from the physical pain on her face.

"Why did you buy me?" she asks.

She chose her question well tonight. And I don't know whether to answer her with the truth or let her commit a sin. I'll give her whichever she needs.

So I take my time, reading her face. She wants the truth, but not all of the truth. She's not ready to face why I bought her. She's not ready to learn I bought her to save her.

She wants the other half of the truth.

She wants me to tell her I want her. I longed for her. I couldn't resist her.

So that's how I answer, "Because I wanted you. I've never wanted anything more. Not another woman. Not money. Not a fancy car. Not an expensive yacht. Not a luxury trip. I've never felt so much want, so much need in my entire life as I did watching you on that stage.

"Even if I didn't have the money to buy you, you were mine from that night. Nothing would have stopped me from claiming you. Not another rich asshole. Not Oscar. Not Julian. Not a calvary of a hundred men. You were mine. And I was yours from the moment I saw you."

It's the first time I've mentioned ever belonging to her as much as she belongs to me. It was a slip of the tongue, but completely true. I've been hers for a lot longer than she's been mine.

A tear drips, slowly at first, then speeds down her cheek as more moisture pushes it faster, and gravity pulls harder.

I reach out and wipe the tear from her eye. It's such a normal act—something any couple would do for the other. But we aren't a couple. She just admitted we will never be.

I was too late.

I don't know if she meant Julian succeeded in raping her before I got there, or if she just meant too much has happened for us to move forward. Maybe she meant she could never forgive me for letting Julian lay a single finger on her. For buying her in the first place. For letting her think I would sell her.

I've sinned too many times for any truth I speak to heal us. Our wounds are too deep. Permanent scars have already formed.

"Your turn," she says with a deep breath.

I pull my hand away from her cheek. And I feel loss. So much loss.

She grips the bedsheets, pulling them tightly to her chest as she waits for my question. I don't know if I want to pull a truth or a sin from her. I want answers, especially after what happened with Julian, but I don't know if I have the strength to hear her past with him. She also, more than anyone, deserves to commit a sin against me.

So I ask the question. The only question I need answered truthfully.

The question that holds my end.

I don't understand how I know, even now, but her truth will change everything.

"How did Julian hurt you before?"

Her eyes drift up to mine, and she bites her lip. I can tell more than ever that she wants to tell me the truth. She wants to pour her soul to me.

And yet there is something stopping her. Something preventing her from screaming the truth.

"Truth or sin?" I ask. *What's it going to be?*

"Sin," she answers.

I suck in a breath, preparing myself for her sin.

She's weak—she shouldn't get out of bed. She might choose to postpone her sin. Or she is going to have to choose something simple she can do from bed.

She pats the side of the bed next to her. Apparently, she's already decided on her sin. She knew before she answered what it was going to be.

I feel a lump in my throat. My heart is racing. My muscles are aching, trying to figure out what she is going to do.

I'm so close to her. I want to kiss her, taste her. I want to worship her body until she begins to forgive me. Until she no longer thinks it's too late to give us a chance.

"What do you want? What's your sin?" I ask, unable to wait, unable to contain myself any longer.

Siren moves hesitantly toward me. Her body inches closer and closer. I prepare myself for a coming slap, punch, or hit. I won't stop her. I deserve any pain she wants to inflict my way.

I try to keep my eyes open. But my reflexes will stop her

if I see it coming, so I sit on my hands and close my eyes and wait.

I breathe slowly in and out, waiting for the pain to hit me. I'm begging it to. *Maybe I'll feel better if I'm hurting even a fraction of the amount she is?*

But what I feel is the opposite of pain.

Her lips brush over mine, ever so slowly, sparking something deep inside, bringing me back to life.

My eyes fly open at her touch. Our eyes lock as her lips hover over mine. I don't move. This is her sin, not mine. But it takes all of my self-control not to devour her.

And then, everything changes. She grabs my neck, pulling my head to her in a forceful kiss I've been dying for since the moment I saw her in the water swimming toward me.

My hands fly up, gripping her head and deepening the kiss. My hungry tongue pushes into her mouth, tasting every drop of her. So sweet, sassy, and delicious.

She moans against my lips, kissing me again and again. With promises of what could be.

These kisses are nothing like I've ever felt before. These kisses are life itself. I hold her firmer, and she tugs hard on my hair, letting it fall down the way she likes.

I could be the man for her. Her beast in the bedroom, her protector during the day. I could give up everything else for her—my job, my friends, my home. I feel it the second our lips touch.

She's everything I've ever wanted, and nothing I knew existed.

When she nibbles on my bottom lip, I'm done. *I'm hers.*

Completely.

Wholly.

Entirely.

Hers.

And she knows it. She smiles back against my lips.

But then she grips my hands, and gently pushes them away from her face, so she can pull back.

I feel empty without her touching me.

"It's too late," she says sharply.

It's then I realize her sin. Siren kissed me, showing me everything I could have. Everything missing from my life. Everything I could have had if I were a better man. Then she took it all away with three little words.

Fuck—this is my life now. I'll forever feel empty without her. There is no going back to a life without her.

I can't have her.

I was too late.

25

SIREN

WHY DID I KISS HIM?

That kiss was painful.

Well, not the kiss part. The kiss part was great. It was magical, passionate, and everything I've been missing.

Cheesy, but it's true.

And now...now, I'm ruined. That kiss ruined me worse than anything Julian could ever do.

We don't speak after my sinful words. We both just collapse into the bed, so close but not touching, as is our life together. Close, but never together.

Not as friends.

Not as lovers.

And soon, not even as enemies.

I don't think I can sleep, but soon the darkness pulls at me. I'm still physically exhausted, so even though I'm anxious, sleep still wins.

I hear a vibrating sound on the dresser.

Zeke jumps out of bed and grabs his phone.

"Yes?" he answers grumpily.

He listens for a minute while looking at me to see if I'm

awake. He must spot the white of my eyes staring back at him because he doesn't stop looking at me.

"Tonight?" he asks.

Fuck, no. He can't go anywhere near Julian. It was just last night that he had to save me from him—that they fought.

But then I notice the rest of the room for the first time. The IV pole, the bags, the medications, the gauze. That's a lot of IV bags if I was just out of it for a day. I've been unconscious for days, possibly weeks.

Which means it's time for Zeke to transport the women. To sell them to the highest bidder. To confirm he is just as bad as Julian.

For a long time, I thought Zeke might be different. The way he treated me these last few days. Nursed me back to health. He's never laid a hand on me, and it makes me believe he is a good guy. Or at least not a bad guy.

But if he sells those women, he's just as evil as Julian. Just as wicked as every other man in my life.

Zeke hangs up the phone, and my attention goes back to him as he walks toward the bed, with indecision in his eyes.

"Don't," I say.

He pauses and looks at me with sadness.

"Don't go. Stay."

His eyes get big as he looks at me. He doesn't nod. He doesn't answer me with words.

And for a moment I think he is going to go—that he's going to leave me.

Instead, he pulls the sheets back and climbs into bed. And then he puts his arm over my body. It's not sexual; he doesn't even pull me to his chest. He just rests his arm over my body with a promise to protect me always.

I wait until he falls asleep for me to close my eyes. And I'm asleep within seconds of my eyelids falling.

But when I wake up, I already know the truth. Zeke is a bad guy. He's a monster. He's gone.

If it wasn't too late before, it is now. I will put up with a lot of things, but not this. *Never this.*

26

ZEKE

THIS ENDS TONIGHT.

The three words play over and over in my head as I slip out of bed in the middle of the night. As I walk quieter than a ghost through my house and out to my truck.

I consider walking the quarter of a mile to Julian's house but think better of it. I might need the truck. And I want to save all my energy for Julian.

Tonight, Julian dies for his sins.

He dies for tying Siren up.

He dies for touching her.

For hitting her.

For almost raping her.

He dies.

The second he chose to touch her; he sealed his fate. Death is all his future can hold. I can't let him breathe another second for what he did to Siren.

Julian ruined the best thing in my life. In one night, he took every chance at happiness away.

Maybe Siren and I still wouldn't have ended up together. But I had hope. Hope for her. For me. And for us.

I could have asked her out on a real date. Brought her flowers every day for a year to apologize for buying her instead of telling her the truth from the start—that I bought her to keep her safe.

Siren could have forgiven me for keeping her in the dark and pretending to be a monster. But she can't forgive me for failing her. She can't forgive me for hurting her.

I was so close to being able to tell her everything. I got rid of the bugs in the house. And I had a plan for how to pay off my debt to Julian without becoming a human trafficker myself. I could have told her the truth. Every move I've made has been to protect her.

Now, that's all gone—because of Julian.

I don't have a shot in hell. Siren deserves better. A man worthy of her. A man with honor and goodness in his heart.

I will never be that man.

Unless killing the bastard who touched her is honorable.

I don't know anymore. I just know it has to be done.

It won't give me any more points in Siren's book. She won't look at me with want in her eyes. She might even hate me for killing yet another man. She may think no one deserves to be slaughtered, even a demon like Julian.

But it has to be done. Julian has to die.

I didn't realize tonight was going to be when he dies until Oscar called, saying the shipment is ready for me. It's been almost two weeks since Julian laid a hand on Siren. She's been sleeping and recovering while I played doctor, hooking up IVs and medications to keep her alive.

Tonight became *the* night the second Oscar called. My time is up. I either kill Julian and every man who works for or with him, or I traffic women.

My choice is easy.

Even if I'll spend the rest of my life running, hunting

down lead after lead, connection after connection of men who work for Julian. Men who, after today, will become my enemy.

I may never return to my previous life. I may never work for Enzo Black again. I may never get to joke with my best friend, Langston. Or see if Kai finally tamed Enzo.

I will live my life alone. My only purpose will be killing and ensuring Siren's safety. I'll have to watch Siren from afar. Watch her get a new job, move into a new place. Date other men. Marry a man. Have kids with another man.

It will be torture, but a worthy life. Because if I have to spend the rest of my life protecting Siren, then my life is worth something. I'll have spent my time on this earth doing something honorable instead of wasting it away, committing the worst crimes.

I pull up in front of Julian's house in my truck. It's the middle of the night, but Julian surely already knows I'm here. He doesn't have the security features my former boss did, but he's paranoid enough to have a solid security system.

He knows I'm here.

I prefer it that way. I don't want to sneak into his bedroom while he's sleeping and shoot him dead. I'm not that kind of guy.

I want a battle.

I want to know the best man won when I kill him.

I want him to look into the whites of my eyes as he bleeds out in front of me.

When I step out of my truck, I slam the door extra hard, ensuring my presence is known, if it wasn't already.

Then I pull out my gun, load it, and cock it. I hold it to my side as I walk calmly to the front door.

I don't ring the doorbell.

Instead, I kick down the double-bolted door with my massive foot and step inside.

My ears are alert, listening for any sign of Julian or his guards. I will have to take out his guards too, but I hope when I finally get to Julian, it will end with just the two of us fighting.

My eyes scan the darkness, and I see a shadow move in the living room.

Cautiously, I hold my gun out as I move through the dark entryway. When I get to the living room, I see Julian seated in a chair towards me, waiting.

Shoot him. Now.

End this.

But something stops me.

And then, it's too late.

The lights flick on, and I see thirty men surrounding Julian.

I don't drop my gun, though. I've been outnumbered before. I have a fifty-fifty chance of winning, killing every bastard here.

If it was just me I had to worry about, I might take those odds. Fifty-fifty is pretty good when it comes to a gunfight. Technically, just fighting a man one on one is fifty-fifty odds, because all it takes is one shot—one bullet to hit me in just the wrong spot for me to lose. But one on one, I've never lost before, so I consider my odds much higher.

But with this many men—fifty-fifty.

There is a fifty-fifty chance I live or die.

A fifty-fifty chance I return to Siren.

A fifty-fifty chance I can protect her.

A fifty-fifty chance Julian finds her and finishes what he started.

I can't take the chance. Because if I fail, Siren is who will pay for my loss, not me. Sure, I'll be dead, I won't even realize I lost. But I won't have to suffer the consequences like she will.

I look around at the thirty men I've never seen before. Julian's operation is bigger than I realized. *Where has he been hiding this army?* They are muscular, confident, and know how to hold a gun from the looks at them. Any one of them could do the job Julian asked of me. *So why does he want me?*

"We've been waiting for you," Julian says, with a grin.

I don't lower my gun, and none of the men draw theirs. It's like they know Julian isn't really in any danger. That's either a mistake on their part or mine.

Fuck—I've already lost.

Julian snaps his fingers and looks at the man on his right. "Load up. Zeke will be right there to lead you."

The men all file out of the room. Now's my chance. It's just me and Julian.

I don't lower the gun, but I don't pull the trigger either. I wouldn't be shocked if Julian already has a man near my house, ready to attack Siren if anything goes wrong tonight.

I put in extra security measures at the house. I even left a gun under Siren's pillow to protect her. But it won't be enough if I don't return.

"I'm done," I say.

I lower my gun. I mean it. Julian still needs to die, but it doesn't have to happen tonight. I have to put Siren first. I have to protect her at all costs, which means returning to her as fast as possible and then getting us off this fucking island.

Julian folds his hands and cocks his head up as he looks at me. "You owe me a debt, Zeke. I saved your life."

I toss my gun in front of him. "And consider this me

saving yours. I should have killed you for what you did. You touched what was mine without permission."

I study his face. His has caked-on makeup to cover the bruising on his face. He's still injured two weeks later.

Good.

I'd rather him be in the hospital right now, or better yet, six feet under. But knowing he's bruised and hurting brings me some level of satisfaction.

Julian shakes his head. "I don't accept."

I frown. "You don't have a choice."

"I have thirty men who say otherwise."

I growl.

"But I'm willing to negotiate; I'm a fair man. I think we can come to an agreement if you want out."

I don't like the sound of this.

"I'll give you a choice for paying your debt off. You can either transport the women to their new owners and ensure we get paid more than a fair amount for each, or you can buy your freedom."

My chest rises and falls heavily. Julian doesn't own me. I shouldn't have to pay for my freedom. But right now, I'll do anything if it means I don't have to fall deeper into the depths of hell.

"How much?"

Julian twists his mouth, thinking for a moment. "Let's see, the going rate for a person seems to be what? Thirty million?"

I narrow my eyes. It's the amount I paid for Siren. He wants me to pay him the same amount to earn my own freedom.

"And since I'll most likely lose my account with Oscar over this, since none of my current men have any brains when it comes to business, I'll require a bonus. Your pet will do."

The money was one thing; adding Siren means the choice isn't even an option. I will never betray Siren again.

Julian grins. "Money and one girl, or you sell two hundred women. I would think the choice is easy since two hundred is more than one. One girl can't mean that much to you, can she?"

Fuck him.

He knows.

He knows I've never touched Siren.

Never fucked her.

He knows I only bought her to save her. And he knows I don't want to sell the other women; I'm not that kind of man. This is a test, and no matter what I choose, I lose.

"Which will it be? Pay for your freedom and give up one girl? Or become the monster you hate and sell two hundred humans into slavery?"

I already know my choice, and I hate it. I hate him. But I never had a choice.

"I need to ensure Siren will be safe. That you won't touch her. No man will."

Julian nods. "What do you want me to do?"

"I already have a new security system in place. I will be able to see everything that goes on inside my house. I want you to place three of your best men on guard outside of the house. I want you to hire a cook and nurse who you trust to cook and take care of Siren while I'm gone."

"Done."

"You won't touch her. You won't go near the house. You will never lay a hand on her again."

"Are you finished?"

"No, I'll do the job. But you won't get the money until I return. Until the job is over, and I know Siren is safe."

Julian frowns. "And if you screw me over, what I did to your pet before will seem kind compared to what I will do."

I suck in a breath. *I can't fail.* If I do, Siren's life will be on the line.

I hold out my hand, and he shakes it.

Then, I turn to find the thirty men who will work for me while I do the job.

A job that will destroy my soul.

A job that will consume my heart.

A job that will turn me into the devil.

I can't save them. That's the lie I keep telling myself. Because I can save them. And two hundred is greater than one, but I choose Siren instead. It's a choice I will never regret.

27

SIREN

It's been twenty-three days.

Twenty-three fucking days.

I haven't heard from Zeke for twenty-three days.

And it's driving me mad.

Sure, he has guards posted outside my window protecting me, but they're probably keeping me inside as much as they are keeping people out.

And sure, I've had a private chef come cook for me the most delicious food every night. He's even been teaching me how to cook.

And yes, a home nurse came over every day to check on me while I was healing. Once I'd healed, she still came to bring me movies, books, and entertainment. She would talk about gossip in town, and the horrible storms we've been having.

But none of that matters. Zeke isn't here.

And I'm trapped in his fucking house.

I don't know what's happening, and yet, I know. He's doing the job Julian asked of him. He's trafficking women.

Even after everything Julian did to me, Zeke is still making that man money.

Fuck him.

He's nothing but a spineless coward. He should have told Julian to go fuck himself, find himself a new number two. Instead, he went in the middle of the night, the second Julian called. Zeke put Julian above me—again.

I'm done. I'm so done. As soon as Zeke gets back, I'm ending this.

I'm done being captive.

I'm done waiting for Zeke to decide what to do with me.

I'm done.

I hear the front door slam shut—Zeke.

He's finally back.

And I'm ready to give him hell.

I run through the house full of rage, ready to tell him off. To demand answers. To finish this.

But I stop in my tracks at the sight of him sitting on the stairs and kicking off his shoes.

Zeke looks horrible, like he hasn't slept in a month. His boots are covered—in mud, blood, water, and god knows what. His jeans are splattered with more dark red spots. His leather jacket has rips in it. And his once white T-shirt looks more gray than white. He now wears a full beard, having not shaved for twenty-three days. And his hair is technically in a man bun, but most of his hair has fallen out, and he hasn't bothered to fix it.

Maybe I shouldn't pounce yet?

I should let him have a day.

A day to shower, eat, sleep.

No.

This is war. He deserves everything that is coming.

"Where the fuck have you been?" I shout, folding my

arms and sticking my hip out as anger consumes me.

Zeke doesn't look up. He just unties his second boot before slipping it off.

"Did you hear me? Or did you lose your hearing the twenty-three days you've been gone?"

His head snaps up—pain. His sight lasers through my heart. He's hurting so fucking much.

Well, too bad. He's not the only one in pain.

"You don't get to just leave me for a month on my own trapped in this house!" I shout, walking toward him.

He stands up. "Watch your mouth, Siren. You have no idea what I've been through."

"I have no idea what you've been through? Are you fucking serious?"

I push him square on the chest. He doesn't move, but it still feels good. Instead, he steps around me.

"I know exactly what you've been through because it's been the only thing I've been thinking of this entire time," I scream.

I follow him, and when he turns down the hallway, I push again. This time, he's off-balance enough to take a small step back.

"You've been tying women up."

Push.

"Threatening their lives with your gun."

Push.

"Locking them up in cages."

Push.

"Transporting them to far off countries in the back of vans and cargo holds."

Push.

"Making calls with the most disgusting men in the world."

Push.

"Negotiating costs and pushing prices higher and higher so you and Julian can make more money."

Push.

Zeke's body is pressed flush against the wall now. I'm unhinged—my body relentlessly pushing his against the wall over and over.

I can't remember being this pissed with a man before. *But why?* He did his job. He's just like Julian and every other man on this island.

Because I was stupid enough to think that Zeke might be better. That he had a speck of good in a sea of bad, but he's just like all the rest.

"Do it," I say, shoving again.

He frowns, not understanding what I'm saying.

"Rape me! Hurt me! Be a fucking man!" I push again. "You've already hurt hundreds of women. I'm not any different than any of them. Stop pretending you are the good guy. You're not a good man. You're evil. The devil!"

Zeke doesn't move, even when I push him again.

My body is boiling. I'm red, exhausted, and angry, but I can't stop. I need this to end. One way or the other, I need this over.

"Stop pretending you need the excuse of the stupid game to sin!" I cry.

This time when I launch myself, my body falls into his. I'm too exhausted to hold myself up anymore. Too angry.

Zeke holds me gently in his arms. My head rests on his chest, and his arms hold me up at the elbows.

We are both still for a moment. I pant heavily against his chest as I watch his rise and fall. My ear is pressed against his pec, and I can hear it—the thumping of his heart. It's accelerated. Beating as fast as mine.

I look up and see the pain on Zeke's face, mixed with desire. He's desperate for me, yet he still exercises restraint.

I'm tired of him being a gentleman to me when he's a monster to everyone else. I need to see the real him. It's the only way.

I lift my head from his chest.

He freezes as if he can read my mind and already knows where this is going. If he just stays still, he'll be able to resist.

But he's a man, a monster—he won't be able to stop himself.

I rise on my tiptoes, and then, I kiss him.

I melt as soon as our lips touch. His are so soft, so welcoming, so *mine*.

Fuck, where did that thought come from?

He tilts his head, letting me in more as his deep voice strains against his vocal cords as I slide my tongue into his mouth.

Yes, stop resisting—show me who you really are.

I grab his neck, holding his lips to me as we kiss harder, our mouths begging for more. For more than a kiss can give.

It's an endless kiss—wet, and hot, and delicious. I love everything about it. How he moves his tongue, how his lips part, even the scruffy hair on his face against my cheeks.

It's what I've been searching for forever. But it's not real. This isn't the real Zeke.

At the same time, we push each other away, until we are arms-length apart.

Our hands still hold each other. His hands claw my shoulders, and mine graze the surface of his biceps. We pant hard and fast. Neither of us is getting enough oxygen right now to think clearly.

"Why did you stop? You know you don't want to," I breathe out.

His eyes turn in his head. He's fighting his self-control—

hard. And his dick is winning.

Yes, just a little more, and I'll have you. You'll show me your true monster, and then I can use it against you. But what will it cost me?

"Why did *you* stop?" He throws my words back at me.

"This isn't about me. This is about you. About the monster you've become."

He shakes his head with a sexy grin as he wipes his mouth with the back of his hand. *Like that's all it takes for him to get rid of me—ha.*

"Oh, beautiful. You really think I'm the only one with a monster inside?" His eyes meet mine. "If I'm a beast, you're a tiger. Just as vicious, just as willing to devour innocent prey."

I narrow my eyes.

And we both attack again.

He goes for my hair; I go for his jacket.

He pulls my hair back, tilting my head as he lays another kiss on my neck as I push his jacket off.

He grabs my neck, pulling me tightly to him, not willing to let me go. I grab the V of his shirt and rip it all the way down the middle until I see his rippling muscles and tattooed body.

His hand tangles into my hair, fisting it back, giving himself better access to my lips. I want more, and so does he.

I grab his scrunchie and rip it out of his hair as he pushes my shirt up as he feels my smooth stomach.

Progress.

But then, he snaps back.

I reach for him, but I feel nothing but air.

He's glued to the wall, his hands stuck to his side.

I laugh. "You afraid?"

"You have no idea," he pants.

I touch my swollen lip with my finger. *I want more. And*

now I'm afraid. Because I'm not supposed to want him back. I'm supposed to be in control. But a few kisses and I want him as badly as he wants me.

"I have an idea." I grab the hem of my shirt and lift it over my head.

He groans at the sight.

He didn't realize I wasn't wearing a bra when his hands were all over my stomach.

His eyes flutter up to the ceiling, as if not looking is going to save him. He already has my body ingrained in his head. There is no escaping.

"Zeke?" I say, my voice dropping to serious levels.

His eyes carefully drop back to me, attempting not to catch a glance of my boobs, of my nipples hardening for his touch.

"Yes?" He answers.

"Kiss me."

We charge at each other. This time he grabs my ass, and my legs wrap around his body. I feel his erection push between my legs; my nipples rub against his chest as our mouths collide.

*This is what has been missing—these kisses. This…*I've never felt whole kissing another man. I've never felt protected and safe. But Zeke forces me to feel all of it.

His lips are evil liars, but incredibly sexy and talented liars.

I'll call him out on the lying later. Right now, I just want to kiss him. Enjoy my last moments of pleasure with this man.

He spins us around, until my back is against the wall, and breaks the kiss far too soon.

I pout.

He chuckles, giving me a wink, before he dips his head

down and finds my nipple.

"Ah, fuck," I moan, holding onto his head to keep him from pulling away again.

I thought his tongue was talented in my mouth, but it's reaching new levels on my nipple. The sensation radiates all over my body. I'm throbbing between my legs, needing so much more than he's currently offering. This can't stop. Not until...

Until I let him fuck me?

Because that can't happen. I can't reward him like that for all the shitty things he's done. Even if it's a reward for myself too.

Once again, Zeke stops.

This time I do too.

What the hell are we doing?

We can't keep doing this.

We hate each other.

We want to destroy each other.

And kiss each other, lick each other, fuck each other...

Zeke rests his forehead against mine as we breathe into each other's mouths. I see and feel the pained expression on his face. It's the same one I wear.

I'm so confused.

He is too.

What are we doing?

No, better question—*what is he doing?* If he wants me, then he has the power to take me. To force me. To take what he wants from me. He paid for it. *So what's stopping him from taking it?*

I don't want him to take anything. Being raped by a man I kinda, sorta find attractive is still a horrible experience. It's still rape. It will still top my list of worst nights.

I reach down between our legs, and find his dick,

squeezing hard.

He howls and shoves me hard against the wall, forcing me to release my grip.

I've awakened the beast with my touch. I can see it in his eyes. I wanted to know who he really is—*this is it.*

This man standing before me, with long, wild hair. An untamed beard. Tattoos covering as many scars as muscle. A ripped body he used to torture, rape, and kill. Life-taking hands. And a brain filled with dirty thoughts about me since the second he bought me.

That's who he is. And he's one push away from acting on it. From proving me right—that he's a monster.

Zeke sees into my mind. He reads my thoughts. And he takes back control.

"What did Julian do to you to make you so scared of him? What did he do to you before?"

I shake my head. "Playing this game doesn't make you any less of a monster. You've wanted to rape me ever since you bought me; just because you've earned the right to commit a sin doesn't make you any less of a sinner."

"Answer the question, and I won't get to sin."

I grit my teeth together. This is the moment. The moment where the truth mixes with sin. This is the moment where I find out the truth of who Zeke really is.

How do I want to learn the truth about him? By speaking my own truth? Or letting him sin?

I'm not ready to share my secret, not until he's spilled his first.

But if I choose sin, will I forever feel guilty for him raping me? Because I gave him the power to do it?

No, I won't. If I choose sin, it doesn't give him permission to violate me in that way. Even if I choose sin, I will still fight back. I won't let him get that far.

"Sin," I answer.

His eyes gloss over with that single word. He needed, and feared, that answer.

Your move, big guy. Your move. Let's see what you got. Because I'm about to castrate you.

My legs are still wrapped around his waist. I'm still gripping his shoulders, but that doesn't mean I've given him permission to fuck me.

Maybe if he asked first, but he won't.

He makes a decision in an instant; then he's carrying me through the foyer. I assume he's going to take me to the bedroom, but he doesn't. He takes me to the living room.

Huh? Not a bed kind of guy? Or does he not want to bother having to change the sheets after the ensuing bloody battle?

He finds the large ottoman in the center of the room, kneels in front of it, and sets my ass down on the edge.

"Lean back," he says.

I frown. If he thinks I'm just going to lay back and take it, he's crazy.

"I said, lay back," his voice deeper, more powerful than before.

I fall back automatically.

Shit, now what?

I slip my hand slowly in the back pocket of my jeans and grab the knife I hid there. I hold it to my back as he unbuttons my jeans and slowly slides them over my hips, then down my body.

I purse my lips and breathe out slowly. *I've got this—he won't touch me without getting castrated.*

Next, he grabs my lacy panties. He takes his time undressing me.

And then I'm naked.

I close my eyes, trying to calm myself. He's still not

undressed, so I have time before he fucks me. He's a slow, gentle giant. He won't speed up just to rape you. He's waited this long. He's a patient man; he'll wait until he's good and ready.

I grip the knife tighter, preparing myself.

I feel his hands on my inner thighs; he gently spreads me apart.

This is it—the moment I need to attack before he does something he can't take back.

"Siren?" he asks.

My eyes open and look at him.

He smirks at me, but his eyes say something else. They ask for permission.

Permission for what?

His eyes dip down, and I realize what he's about to do. His jeans are still on. His hands have my legs spread, and his face is positioned just over my pussy, ready to devour me.

He wants to fuck me with this mouth, not rape me. That's his sin—giving me pleasure.

I blink several times, completely confused.

How could this be? How is he this guy, not the monster? Or is he only this guy when he's around me? And he's a monster around everyone else?

Zeke hovers over me, waiting for some sign of permission. Technically he never asked with words, but we've never needed words to communicate.

Yes—no.

How do I decide? My body is begging me to let him kiss me there. I already know it will be the most explosive orgasm of my life. *But is that giving in? Being weak? I shouldn't—*

But I feel my hips move up on their own accord.

Zeke grins broader before he licks his lips.

Wait, I didn't answ—

His tongue licks over my slit, and I realize my hips made a much better choice than my brain would. One stroke of his tongue and I'm his. I don't care what he's done. I don't care how evil his heart is. I don't care how many people he's killed or how many lives he's stolen.

Feeling his tongue between my legs, over my most sensitive area while he kneels in front of me, expecting nothing from me in return, is everything I've ever wanted in a man.

And god is it sexy to see him giving instead of taking from me.

I lean up on my elbows so I can watch him lick me. At first, he's slow, so achingly slow. But it only intensifies everything. I can feel every lick, flick, and breath coming from his mouth.

And then he narrows in on my clit.

Too much. My legs close in around his head.

He grins as he licks over my clit more, and his hands slowly spread me wide for him again.

"I think your clit likes my tongue," he says.

"Mmm," is my response.

"Keep your legs spread, or I'll stop," he commands.

I frown. That's an impossible task, but I see why he commands it from me. He removes one hand from my leg and puts two of his fingers in his mouth before I feel them pushing at my entrance.

I tighten at first, resisting anything entering. *It's been a long time, too long.*

He removes one finger and tries again, being so slow and patient with me, waiting until my body accepts him before he pushes.

He licks faster, moving out of his usual slow movements

for me. I arch, my muscles relax, and his finger glides inside me.

"Fucking, wow," I get out.

"If you think that was good, just wait. I'm about to have you screaming and cursing my name."

I like his promise. And I can't wait for him to deliver on it.

He slides his finger out, and I curse the emptiness I feel. I want him inside me—more than just his finger, but I'm not ready to tell him that yet.

He starts pushing in again, but this time a second finger joins in. I feel an intense tightness as he pushes further.

"Relax, baby," he whispers over my clit, licking faster.

I look at his eyes. They scream, begging—*trust me.*

I do. Fuck, I do.

I let go.

Of my expectations.

My fears.

My observations.

My pain.

My truth.

I'm just here, with a man doing incredible things to my body.

As soon as I let go, Zeke takes complete control. His fingers thrust inside me with expert ability. His tongue licks and nips at my clit. And his eyes promise me the world.

Our eyes lock until I can't look at him any longer. Everything is too intense.

And then I explode all at once, throwing my head back and clamping my eyes closed. My back arches, my toes curl, and my legs tighten around his head. My pussy clenches down in a ripple of throbs, releasing my orgasm on his fingers.

What. Just. Happened?

My brain seems to thaw, and my first thought is blissful bewilderment.

I smile up at the world, because for the first time, it brought me something good. Even if it was only supposed to last for this short time, I wouldn't trade a single bad thing in my life if it meant giving up these few minutes with Zeke.

I hear him moving.

I sit up, and then he's draping a throw blanket over my shoulders. He scoops me up, and we move to the couch before he sets me down on his lap.

His eyes drop down to my lap.

Mine follow.

"Oh, um..." I start, trying to explain why I'm gripping a knife.

He chuckles. "If you castrate me, I deserve it." He leans forward and kisses my forehead sweetly. I can smell myself on his breath. *Jesus, I smell delicious on his face.*

I expect him to try and take the knife from me; he doesn't.

Slowly, I come back to life. To the real world. And he just gave me the most beautiful sin. It felt dirty, wrong, but oh-so-delightful.

I consider thanking him, but it doesn't feel right, so I don't. But I do have my question. I know what I want to ask him.

"Who are you, Zeke? A beast or a monster?"

He tucks my hair behind my ear as he grips my neck, stroking me with his thumb.

"Is there a difference?" he asks hesitantly, afraid I'll say no.

"Yes."

He nods and then leans back against the couch. I tighten

the blanket around me. I hold my breath, waiting for his answer. *Will he choose beast or monster?* If he says monster, there is no saving him. He's cruel down to the bone. And this ends here.

But if he says beast, it will give me hope. Beauty was able to tame the beast in the end. The beast had a heart. The beast could still love, even though he sometimes did cruel things. And that makes all the difference to our future.

"Sometimes, I'm afraid that I'm a monster."

I suck in a breath—*dammit.*

"But after spending time with you, I've realized I'm a beast."

I smile—*yes, my beast. My gentle giant. My anchor, keeping me calm and protected while I wait out the storm.*

I got my answer.

But Zeke doesn't stop there. He tells me his whole truth.

"I lived in Miami. I was born in New York, but I moved to Miami shortly after. I worked for..."

No. Please, no. Don't say it.

"Enzo Black. He was my best friend and boss. We mainly handled security and created super-yachts for our rich clients. But during my time with him, I did horrible things. I stole, threatened, killed. But every time it was to protect my boss, my friends."

No...my heart is breaking.

"I almost died saving them."

No, no, no.

He tucks a finger under my chin.

I can't breathe.

"Until you. You saved me."

I exhale. *I can't do this.*

"I owe my life to you, not Julian."

But I have to.

"So when we met again, when your life was threatened to be taken, about to be sold, I knew what I had to do. I had to save you."

My heart shatters with his words. Because a part of me hoped he was cruel. Hoped I was wrong about him. Pleaded he didn't buy me to protect me.

"Maybe I did it the wrong way. I should have told you the truth sooner. But I bought you to save you, to protect you from the other men."

Zeke is a good person. He's my protector. My savior. I just wish I could say the same thing about myself.

"At first, I couldn't tell you the truth. Julian had everything bugged. He could listen to our conversations, but I removed all the eavesdropping devices."

I close my eyes as tears fall—warm, wet, salty tears.

Zeke being Zeke, the amazing man he is and I always suspected was beneath his shell, wipes my tears away.

"Now, I can complete my promise. Now, I can save you."

There is so much promise in his words—so much genuine affection. I swear I even see a hint of love in his eyes when he looks at me.

And it hurts, god does it hurt.

I swallow back my tears, wiping them on the back of my hand.

Because just like that, my high crashes down.

My world ends.

Whatever we had for a splitting moment is over.

Zeke finally spilled his truth.

Which means it's my turn to spill mine.

Mine is half-truth, half-sin. Mine is going to fucking hurt —leave a permanent scar where our hearts once were.

But I no longer have a choice between truth or sin. Now I must do both.

28

ZEKE

ONE SECOND, I'm spilling my heart to her, one word away from saying I love her, and the next Siren has me pinned to the floor.

She's naked still, and I'm only wearing my jeans, but the move isn't sexual. It isn't foreplay. *It fucking hurts.*

She's straddling me at the waist, with one of my arms pinned above my head, and her knife at my throat.

My eyes widen, searching for truth in her tear-stained eyes. If she could pull a move like this the entire time, why didn't she? *How did she let men kidnap her in the first place? Why didn't she fight harder against Julian? Against me before now?*

I breathe heavily, about to move my free hand when she presses the knife deeper into my neck.

"I'm so sorry," Siren whispers as one tear falls.

I frown. "You have nothing to be sorry for."

She shakes her head, barely holding herself together while physically stronger than I've ever seen her. I notice new muscles in her arms. Her thighs clench my waist hard, holding me down.

"Zeke, I—" Siren starts.

Lone, slow clapping cuts her off.

Siren doesn't look, she just closes her eyes tightly and takes a deep breath as if preparing herself.

I cut my eyes toward the sound.

Julian Reed.

What the fuck is he doing here now?

My eyes look up at Siren, who is still pouring herself into me. Whatever she is pissed at me for will have to wait, we have bigger fish to fry.

Apparently, she disagrees or doesn't read my face, because she doesn't release the knife or let me up.

"Good job, Aria," Julian says.

Siren's head drops.

I look from her to Julian.

"What?" I whisper to Siren. "What did he just call you?"

She swallows. "By my name," she says solemnly.

My mouth falls. *Siren isn't her real name—Aria is.*

Julian walks over to us, looking down at the situation.

"So you work for Enzo Black, huh?" he asks.

I don't answer. Instead, I glare back.

He smirks. "You thought you had removed all the bugs from the house." He laughs and pets Aria's head. "You didn't know I had a plant on the inside switching all the bugs back on as soon as you thought you had disconnected them."

What?

Siren drops her head in disgust but doesn't dispute him.

"She works for me," Julian says, finishing the missing pieces of the puzzle.

"And she's gotten me all the information I needed. You would have never told me who you worked for. And it's even better than I imagined. You work for the great Enzo Black."

Julian's eyes grow greedy. "And now I have the key to bringing Mr. Black down."

"I will never help you," I growl.

He laughs. "I think you will. I got you to spill all your secrets to my beauty here; I think I can convince you to do just about anything."

I look up at Siren, no Aria, and my passion for her has been swapped for anger. She betrayed me. I trusted her. I could have loved her.

"What does he have over you? Why are you working for him?" I ask, pleading Siren, giving her one more chance to tell me differently.

"Because of what he gives me," she answers.

Julian laughs. "You think I force her? Aria is in complete control of her life. I could never force her to do anything she didn't want to do."

I frown, but I see the truth on her face.

Julian looks to Aria. "Lock him up. We have more work to do taking down Enzo Black."

"Yes, sir," she answers, not moving as Julian leaves the two of us.

"You lied to me," I say.

She shakes her head. "I never lie. I always tell the truth."

"Then explain this! You even lied about your name." I spit back.

"I never said 'siren' was my name, just who I was. You took it to mean what you wanted."

"That's still a lie."

"No, it's lying while telling the truth. I warned you. I'm a siren. I lure men to their deaths. You just didn't heed the warning."

She's right. I didn't.

"You thought I was a monster this whole time?" I ask.

She shakes her head. "I hoped, because then this wouldn't be so bad. But I knew in my heart you weren't. That's why I created this plan. I knew you wouldn't be able to let me be sold to another man."

I frown.

"But you aren't a saint. You sold those women," she spits in my face, her face red and angry, trying to rationalize her actions against me now.

I shake my head. "I didn't sell them. I made sure they were safe. Every. Single. One."

Her eyes widen in pain.

Good, she deserves it.

"I could have saved you too," I whisper.

"Not when I didn't want to be saved."

"Did Julian hurt you? Is that why you work for him?"

She doesn't answer at first. But then she answers with her actions. I don't know how such a tiny body packs such a big hit. I'm seeing stars before I realize she's punched me. And I'm in handcuffs before I try to strike back.

"How the...?"

Her lips thin into a grimace. "I've trained my entire life for a job like this. I take down men. Usually bad guys. Too bad you aren't as bad as all the rest. Because your fate will be the same."

I realize she has my gun on me. She has all the weapons.

"Head downstairs," she says.

I don't move.

"Go. Downstairs. Or I'll shoot you," she says.

"I don't believe you."

She fires but misses on purpose.

I grunt and decide right now isn't the best time to fight. I'm distracted, and I'm not sure I could hurt her even if I had a clear head. Moments ago, I was giving her the best orgasm of her life, although I'm sure that was a lie too.

When I get to the basement, I see the cage. The cage I could have used on her when I bought her, but didn't. I was good to her, too good.

"Inside," she says.

I walk inside. She slams the barred door shut and locks it. Only then does she drop the gun.

"What did Julian do to you?" I ask, needing this answer. Needing her to be honest. I think back through our history. She's an excellent manipulator, and she's right, I don't think she ever spoke a lie.

She told the truth, I was just too stupid to read between the lines. To realize there was a reason she wasn't like every other woman on that stage—because she wasn't really being sold. She wasn't ever in danger. She was just doing her job—undercover, working for one of the cruelest men I've ever met.

"He saved me," she finally answers.

My eyes shoot up.

"Then why did he hurt you?" I ask. I know that was real. I saw the pain she felt. I nursed her back to health. Those were real bruises and scars. Those were real tears she cried.

"I'm not the one who needs saving, Zeke," she says, backing away. She walks upstairs and closes the basement door, leaving me alone in the dark.

Siren's right, she doesn't need saving. And even if she does, I won't be the one to rescue her. I need to save myself.

Unfortunately, Siren has had me under her spell since the moment she saved me. Apparently, she goes around saving men who she thinks her boss will want dirt on. She probably got paid for my secrets more than I paid to buy her.

Her words, though, will stay with me forever—her beautiful voice. I close my eyes, and I can hear them again.

"I always tell the truth, even when I lie."

She warned me, and I fell into her trap. *What other lies were hidden in her truths? What other sins?*

It shouldn't matter. I should escape. Run. Return to my old life. Warn my boss about Julian. Forget about Siren.

But I can't stop thinking about her. My cock can't stop wanting her. And my heart, the stupid muscle that it is, still beats for her. *Stupid, stupid heart.*

Siren saved me, only to use me for her own gain. I pull on the bars. They don't budge.

Now I'm the one in need of saving.

The End

Thank you so much for reading! Zeke and Siren's story continues in Twisted Vow!

Grab the entire Sinful Truths series below!

Sinful Truth #1
Twisted Vow #2
Reckless Fall #3
Tangled Promise #4
Fallen Love #5
Broken Anchor #6

Read Enzo and Kai's story below in the Truth or Lies series! (You also get to read Zeke's beginning)

Taken by Lies #1
Betrayed by Truths #2
Trapped by Lies #3
Stolen by Truths #4
Possessed by Lies #5
Consumed by Truths #6

FREE BOOKS

Read **Not Sorry** for **FREE**! And sign up to get my latest releases & updates here→EllaMiles.com/freebooks

Follow me on BookBub to get notified of my new releases→Follow on BookBub Here

Join Ella's Bellas FB group to grab my **FREE** book **Pretend I'm Yours**→Join Ella's Bellas Here

ORDER SIGNED PAPERBACKS

I love putting my signed paperbacks on SALE!

Check them out by visiting my website:
https://ellamiles.com/signed-paperbacks

Dirty Revenge

Dirty: The Complete Series

ALIGNED SERIES:

Aligned: Volume 1 (Free Series Starter)

Aligned: Volume 2

Aligned: Volume 3

Aligned: Volume 4

Aligned: The Complete Series Boxset

UNFORGIVABLE SERIES:

Heart of a Thief

Heart of a Liar

Heart of a Prick

Unforgivable: The Complete Series Boxset

MAYBE, DEFINITELY SERIES:

Maybe Yes

Maybe Never

Maybe Always

Definitely Yes

Definitely No

Definitely Forever

STANDALONES:

Pretend I'm Yours

Finding Perfect

Savage Love

Too Much

Not Sorry

ABOUT THE AUTHOR

Ella Miles writes steamy romance, including everything from dark suspense romance that will leave you on the edge of your seat to contemporary romance that will leave you laughing out loud or crying. Most importantly, she wants you to feel everything her characters feel as you read.

Ella is currently living her own happily ever after near the Rocky Mountains with her high school sweetheart husband. Her heart is also taken by her goofy five year old black lab who is scared of everything, including her own shadow.

Ella is a USA Today Bestselling Author & Top 50 Best-selling Author.

Stalk Ella at:
www.ellamiles.com
ella@ellamiles.com